THE
NOWHERE
GIRL

LINDA NEWBERY

SCHOLASTIC

For Linda Sargent

Scholastic Children's Books, Commonwealth House,
1–19 New Oxford Street,
London WC1A 1NU, UK
a division of Scholastic Ltd
London – New York – Toronto – Sydney – Auckland
Mexico City – New Delhi – Hong Kong

First published in the UK by Scholastic Ltd, 1997
This edition, 1999

Text copyright © Linda Newbery, 1997

ISBN 0 439 01119 1

Typeset by DP Photosetting, Aylesbury, Bucks
Printed and bound in Great Britain by
Mackays of Chatham plc, Chatham, Kent

2 4 6 8 10 9 7 5 3 1

1. Sidestepping

The sounds of the night ferry lap and throb, waves of sound, waves of water, in and beneath consciousness, pulsing through Cass's dreams as she sleeps fitfully. Tight in the sleeping bag, her limbs want to stretch out at full length. The reclining chair supports her at an angle between sitting and lying, uncomfortable for real sleep. She is hot and restricted in the quilted bag. Waking each time to the deep, mesmerizing throb of engines, she feels the clutch of fear at her throat as she imagines the whole ship tilting, sliding, ceilings becoming walls and walls floors, hundreds of passengers captive in panic. She has made the crossing so often that she shouldn't be afraid, but the names *Estonia* and *Herald of Free Enterprise* haunt her each time. It is unlucky even to think of them, those doomed names.

Around her, in reclining chairs and on the floor, some of the sleeping bags are as still as chrysalises, with only a tuft of hair or an emerging hand to indicate life inside. Elsewhere there are plaid blankets, spread coats. Through the glass Cass sees a sliver of moon, ragged strips of cloud, and the lightening gunmetal grey of the sky. Night is sliding into morning. If she went up to the passenger deck she would be able to see the Normandy coast.

She lies awake, lacing her fingers behind her head. These crossings between Portsmouth and Ouistreham are her transition from Englishness to Frenchness. Late last night, waiting for the ship to sail, she asked for coffee in English.

This morning, in the bleary-eyed pre-dawn café, she will speak French. She is thinking in French. Somewhere in mid-Channel, Cass steps aside to make way for Cécile. She will still call herself Cass but inside she will know she is Cécile.

There is a difference this time, though. Usually, on regular holidays with her parents, it is a game, playing at being Cécile because she knows she will swap easily back to Cass on the return journey. This time, she isn't sure when the return journey will be. In the summer? In the autumn? Never? As far as her friends and family are aware, this is a break: time to herself, a working holiday before she goes back to rejoin the sixth form in September. *Break*. Maybe the term is more appropriate than they realize. Maybe a break is what she wants: a complete break. Maybe she will stay in France, stay Cécile.

Cass is Cécile Angélique Sutherland, an awkward amalgamation of French and English, Cass for short. She hasn't called herself Cécile since starting primary school and being called Cecil by the other children, who thought it a huge joke. Her name is Cass now. Her mother doesn't like it: "Cécile is a lovely name. Cass sounds like something out of a Western." But nevertheless she too calls Cass Cass, except when they visit relations in France. Mum's name is Thérèse, but most English people pronounce it *Trays*.

Cass lifts her head from her rucksack-pillow and feels in the side pocket for her keys. She has to keep checking. She pulls them out so that she can feel their reassuring weight in her hand. Her car keys. Her own car. She thinks of the yellow Fiat Panda down there on the car deck between big holiday-going Rovers and Volvos. She wants to go and release it from the echoey fume-filled layer of ship, drive it out into France.

Having her car makes her feel less lonely than she otherwise would. It is her own, a small piece of mobile territory. The freedom it gives her is still an exciting novelty.

People are beginning to stir. Cass wriggles out of her sleeping bag, rolls and bundles it into its cover, and goes along to one of the washrooms. She has to pick her way over sleeping bodies. In the corridor she tries to close her nostrils to the sweet sickly odour of vomit. Hurrying past, she finds a free toilet cubicle and runs hot water.

When she has finished, she pushes her washing things into her rucksack. Her fingers meet the cool smoothness of paper, enclosing card. She knows what's in the envelope but she can't help taking it out for another look. Monet's *Water Lilies*, and inside the card: "Don't forget to phone and write. Often. I'll miss you. *Je t'aime*. Robbie."

The handwriting is large and sprawling, like Robbie himself. Cass closes the card but then flicks it open for another brief look before replacing it in its envelope and sliding it down inside the rucksack. Typical of Robbie to come up with a last-minute emotional plea. He has never before told her that he loves her, in person or in writing, in French or in English. Now she will feel guilty if she doesn't phone or write, but – at the moment – she doesn't intend to. Maybe a postcard or two, but nothing more. It is partly because of Robbie that she's here at all. A break. A full-stop, or only a comma or semi-colon? She isn't sure. But it won't be a break if she's on the phone every night or writes him daily letters. They have never had that sort of closeness and it certainly isn't the time now. She wants to leave Robbie behind. Robbie is Cass's boyfriend, not Cécile's.

It's too early for breakfast but she buys herself coffee and sits at one of the café tables. France is sliding closer: a pale slick of sand, dawn light washing over the low cliffs and turning the sea to gold. These were the D-Day landing beaches, Sword and Juno. Cass used to play here as a child and it was only later that she learned to associate this stretch of coast with black-and-white footage of helmeted figures rising from the sea, rifles held aloft. Before, the German pill-boxes had been play castles and the memorials no more significant than mile-posts.

If it hadn't been for the war, Cass would be a French girl living in France and attending a French *lycée*. Before the Germans came, her grandparents left for England. She has grown up knowing that, feeling the lure of France tugging her back to her other life. It is always there as an alternative.

Announcements over the tannoy, in French and then in English. Cass goes down to the car deck and squeezes through the narrow gaps between parked vehicles, to her own car and her own driving seat. Holding the steering-wheel gives her confidence. She spreads out her road map on the passenger seat and stows her rucksack behind. Ahead, the ramps are down, stewards waving the cars forward, the reflective strips on their coats catching the light so that they appear to move like disjointed puppets. Cass turns the key, relieved that the ignition starts first time. It sometimes lets her down and it would be embarrassing here, with all the holiday people stuck behind her, impatient to enter the French morning. She hears a metallic *thunk* as the car rolls over the ramp and passes out of the cave of the ship's interior into sunlight. On through Passport Control, a quick flash of the photograph that hardly resembles her at all, and out of the harbour, beneath the signs for CAEN and TOUTES DIRECTIONS. Cass feels excited by her independence – alone in France, mobile, the whole continent stretched out in glistening light like an invitation, offering infinite choice. In fact, she isn't going far, only to St Privat, not far from Bayeux, and at this early hour there is no need to hurry. First, she will enjoy the illusion of being free to go anywhere she chooses.

She has never driven on the right before, although she is used to being a passenger. The route signs are familiar, welcoming: motorway signs in blue, the names of major towns in green, smaller places indicated by clusters of white arrows. The first roundabout unnerves her, having to go round the wrong way. She expects fast traffic to hurtle at her from all directions, angry horns beeping. But the road is quiet at this hour and the only other traffic is from the ferry, mostly British drivers who are also having to adjust. Most head towards Caen and the main routes but Cass turns away from the estuary and takes one of the quiet lanes that border the coast.

A few miles along the shore she parks in a village and gets out. It's full daylight now, bright and blustery. The village is a small settlement like many others along this stretch of coast – a square with a *Bar-Tabac* on one corner and a D-Day memorial opposite, a big church with closed doors painted dark red, a sign to the *Bureau de Poste*. A woman walks neatly along the pavement in high-heeled shoes, well wrapped up, carrying two baguettes. A stony track leads down to the shore, and surrendering to sea, with a row of bungalows as the last barricade. As Cass follows it, the sky opens up big and wide, dazzling her with brightness. She walks along the sea wall until she reaches a concrete slipway to the beach and then she runs down, buffeted by the wind, hair blowing in her face. At the shoreline, the undertow makes the pebbles hiss and roll back. Although it is April the wind is cold, cutting in across the sea, knifing between layers of clothing. Cass's sweater isn't enough and she hugs her arms round her. She can't see the English coast from here and suddenly the immensity of sea and sky is frightening, daunting. It's too lonely here, although loneliness is what she wants.

Abruptly, tiredness overwhelms her and she wants nothing more than to lie down and sleep. Partly the result of her disturbed night, but only partly. "It's like that, getting over glandular fever," Dad has told her. He should know, having had it himself in his teens. "Takes it out of you."

It has certainly taken something out of Cass. Energy, the will to rouse herself to do anything. Easier just to drift, to sleep, to see what happens. And it has taken her out of school. That is the most liberating and the most disturbing thing of all. Liberating, because she is suddenly off the yearly treadmill of lessons, coursework deadlines and exams. Disturbing, because all her friends are still there, getting ahead of her, thinking about their lower sixth exams and their predicted final grades. Cass has missed so much school that if she goes back she will have to start in the sixth form all over again. Going back to school at all would be hard enough, but dropping down a year would make it ten times as difficult. She would have to fit into the year below, make new friends, explain why she's there, while her own friends – the ones she has been with since starting in year seven – surge on ahead to A-levels and applications for university or jobs.

"Make the most of it," her teachers said. "Use the time to do some background reading. Give yourself a head start in September."

She doesn't want a head start. That makes it sound like a race, jostling for position. She doesn't even want to compete. Especially not now, since the crisis with Robbie.

By now she is hungry as well as cold, her stomach churning. She walks back to the village square, thinking of hot coffee and breakfast.

Only the *Bar-Tabac* and the *boulangerie* are open at this early hour. Farther along the street is a *charcuterie*, its blinds still down. Cass pushes open the glass door of the *Bar-Tabac*. Inside, two elderly men sit at the bar, smoking and talking to the proprietor. The room smells of coffee and cigarette smoke. It is a small place, basic but clean, with four plastic-topped tables and a pinball machine. Cass asks for coffee and croissants and sits at the table nearest the window. She soon realizes that the men at the bar have seen the Fiat outside and assume from its British number plate that she's English, even though she ordered her breakfast in French. Her accent is perfect but they probably think she has polished up schoolgirl French for the occasion. They are talking about her in low voices.

"On her own?"

"Looks in need of warming-up."

"I wouldn't mind – if I were thirty years younger –"

Cass realizes that a French girl her age wouldn't go alone into a bar like that, not in a quiet village, where the bar is still largely a male preserve. It would be different in a city or big town. But she is too cold and hungry to mind. The coffee is good and strong and the croissants hot, with creamy Normandy butter melting into the centres. Croissants are never the same in England.

She feels better as the coffee warms her. Strength and optimism return, the feeling of independence reasserts itself. She can go where she wants, buy food for herself when she is hungry. And she has a job to go to at St Privat, with a flat to live in.

In some ways she feels older than her friends at home, in spite of having fallen behind at school. Perhaps because of it. They are still in uniform, going into assembly, sitting in class, handing in their homework. She warms her hands on her coffee cup and looks out at the sunlit square, and thinks that after all she would rather be here.

2 . Le Clos d'If

The house is called Le Clos d'If. Courtyard of the yew. From the road it is a closed, private place behind high railings, giving no glimpse of the space behind which Cass knows is there: gardens, fenced paddocks, the swampy area that is now a bird reserve. The house is early nineteenth-century, slate-roofed and shuttered, L-shaped round its gravel court. There are steps up to the front door and all the windows have heavy net curtains as well as shutters. The yew tree which gives the house its name casts inky shadows over the lawn and reaches out towards the windows on that side as if trying to shield them from the daylight.

If. Yew. As a child, Cass used to play with the words, mixing languages. If yew. If you. If you what? She used to imagine a question mark hanging over the house, as if it posed an unsolvable puzzle.

She parks the car and gets out. Set into an alcove in the wall, like a small shrine, is a Madonna figurine, with a vase of spring flowers at its feet. Cass used to imagine that its eyes followed her wherever she went, seeing any naughty things she did out of sight of the grown-ups. She used to see it as a sort of conscience.

The Fiat looks too small and too yellow, like a toy car left in the courtyard by a child. Cass wonders what it's doing here. Tante Eugénie and Oncle Gérard, Monsieur and Madame Martineau, are her great-aunt and uncle, although it's years since she has been here with Mum and Dad and then only for dinner, never to stay. The place looks more austere than she remembers, even though her memories aren't particularly cosy ones: formal meals in the high-ceilinged dining-room, bored by grown-up conversation, asking to get down from the table and being warned not to touch any of the valuable ornaments. Cass has always sensed her mother's reluctance to come here, her relief when they drive away. The visits are made for duty, not pleasure – squeezed in before the night ferry home. It's difficult for Dad, too, with his limited French, to follow the conversation: he joins in haltingly and ungrammatically when required to, but it's impossible not to leave him out.

Cass's mother didn't want her to come here for the summer. Her face was tight and anxious when Cass showed her the letter from Tante Eugénie, written in a formal looped script.

"You don't want to go, do you? You'll be bored. It'll be lonely there with no one your own age. Eugénie and Gérard are older than Grandmère – in their *seventies* – and twice as staid."

"I don't mind that," Cass said. "I want to go somewhere completely different. I like Normandy and I don't mind if it's quiet and peaceful. That's what I want."

"Let Cass make up her own mind," Dad said, patting his wife's shoulder as if she were a nervous dog.

There is always an air of restraint, almost timidity, about Mum. Cass puts this down to her mother's age: she and Dad were in their late thirties when Cass was born and are now at least ten years older than most of her friends' parents. Amy's and Robbie's parents talk about their hippy days in the early seventies; Mum and Dad can remember post-war poverty,

Bing Crosby and the arrival of television. Dad is young and energetic for his fifty-odd years, while Mum is fading and greying, the careful routines of middle age fixing themselves around her. She always points out the risks and drawbacks of any decision and worries every time Cass goes out at night. Robbie's family is far more easy-going: people come and go, dogs bark, doors slam, Robbie shouts out "Back later!" as he leaves the house for some party somewhere, and no one worries. Perhaps that's one of the attractions of Robbie: his noisy, friendly house.

Was one of the attractions.

Walking up to the front door, Cass feels as if she's about to introduce herself to complete strangers. She reminds herself that Tante Eugénie and Oncle Gérard have been kind enough to offer her work and a home. All the same, she is glad that she won't be living with them in the house. It would be too claustrophobic. She feels like a small child again.

The doorbell has a powerful jangle that seems to echo to the far corners of the house. It is Tante Eugénie who comes to the door. She is tall, a little stooped, as smartly dressed as Cass remembers. She wears a high-necked blouse and a two-piece knitted suit, lavender-coloured, and her feet are pinched into black court shoes. For a moment her blue-grey eyes rest sternly on Cass's face, unrecognizing. Then she realizes, and steps forward to clasp Cass by both shoulders and scan her face eagerly.

"Cécile, my dear!" She kisses Cass on both cheeks, awkwardly, as if she isn't used to shows of affection. Sweet-smelling face powder lingers after the kiss, and the musk of perfume. "You're so like your mother!"

"Really?" Cass thinks she is more like her father – tall, with reddish fair hair and grey eyes. Her mother is smaller and neater.

As Tante Eugénie moves apart her manner becomes more distant, as if she has surprised herself with the effusive gesture. "You must have had a tiring journey, all alone," she says, smoothing the front of her blouse. "Come and meet Gérard."

She leads Cass through a wood-panelled entrance hall and into the sitting-room. Oncle Gérard rises from an upright chair and kisses her, too. He is a short, stocky man with a clipped moustache; his kiss smells of tobacco. He moves stiffly, swinging his left leg from the hip. Cass remembers that he has arthritis, as well as a weak heart. That's partly why she's here, because Oncle Gérard is no longer fit enough to look after the grounds or the animals himself. Tante Eugénie has never had anything to do with the horses.

"You're lucky to have a car of your own, at your age," Oncle Gérard remarks.

"Yes, I know. Mum and Dad bought it for me after I was ill."

"Generous," Tante Eugénie says. Cass detects slight disapproval.

"Yes. But you know what a worrier Mum is. She hates the thought of me travelling by bus late at night or getting lifts. She thinks I'm safer with my own transport."

"It'll make it easy for you to get about during your time off," Oncle Gérard says. "The bus service here is dreadful."

Cass wonders whether they are going to invite her to sit down, or offer her a drink. The sitting-room is elegantly comfortless and very tidy – no trace of a book or magazine, or a cat sitting on the cushions. She wonders what they were doing before she arrived. Through the hallway she can see a table set for dinner.

"Gerard will show you to your *apartement*," Tante Eugénie says. "But tonight you will eat with us. And we would like you to join us for our meal every Sunday after church."

Cass goes out to the car with Oncle Gérard, feeling uneasy. That sounds as if Tante Eugénie expects her to go to church with them. She must surely know that Cass hasn't been brought up as a Catholic, although Mum sometimes attends. Cass doesn't go to church of any sort and isn't going to start now. But explanations will have to wait.

"You might as well park round by the stables," Oncle Gérard says. "It's nearer."

She gets in and starts the engine and follows the swing and lurch of his walk, along a gravel track beside the house, through shrubbery to the stone stable-block. There are post and railed paddocks beyond and Cass can see horses grazing in the dusk, a foal sprawled in sleep. She parks outside the yard gate and opens the hatchback to take out her bags.

"My horses," Oncle Gérard says, nodding towards the paddock. "And a visiting mare, that one with the foal. Tomorrow I will show them to you. But there is no time now before dinner."

Cass would prefer to see the horses now and then eat bread and cheese in her flat, but Tante Eugénie hasn't really left her the choice. Oncle Gérard takes one of her bags from her and opens a wooden door between stables to reveal a narrow flight of stairs.

"There are two flats here," he says. "Yours is the smaller

one. The other is family size. We have an English family coming tomorrow to stay for a fortnight."

Cass hasn't realized there will be other people here. She has noticed the *Gîtes de France* sign at the front gate and thought it referred to the flat she would be having. She wasn't expecting to have English neighbours.

Oncle Gérard unlocks the door and carries the bag inside. The flat is small with sloping eaves, all newly-decorated, light and airy and very different from the gloomy splendour of the main house. Cass goes to the window and looks out over the paddocks. Beyond, she can see the willowy scrubland of the bird reserve, and the glimmer of light on water. She breathes the air of her new home and feels herself relaxing, shedding the tension of her arrival. She will like living here.

"Thank you. It's lovely!" she says. Oncle Gérard shows her the neat kitchen, the shower cubicle, the double bedroom, storage space in the eaves for her bags. In the small refrigerator someone has put a carton of milk, a Camembert cheese, six eggs and a bottle of white wine. There is a jug of cowslips on the window-sill. The kitchen smells freshly cleaned and she wonders who got it ready for her. She can't imagine Tante Eugénie doing it.

"There's a washing machine and ironing-board in the room next to the feed store, down in the yard. I'll leave you to settle yourself in," Oncle Gérard says. "We have dinner at eight o'clock."

Cass is hungry already. While she unpacks, she can't resist eating two of the biscuits she bought earlier at the *Stoc* supermarket outside Bayeux. She looks in the kitchen cupboards and finds an amazing variety of gadgets and utensils, including a coffee filter, a double steamer and a mould in the shape of a fish. She doesn't expect to be doing any elaborate cookery herself but perhaps the holiday visitors like to have the chance. Her aunt and uncle could get a lot of money from renting this flat to visitors if she weren't in it, she realizes; two people, every week throughout the season. And they're going to pay her a small wage as well, pocket money for food and extras. She hopes the work she does for them is going to be worth it. Especially as she isn't a hundred per cent fit, and the work will be physical.

She looks out of the window at the horses in the paddocks. Somewhere beneath she hears the stamp of a hoof on concrete, and then a shuddering snort. Not all the horses are out at grass, then. She remembers that Tante Eugénie's letter mentioned a stallion. Cass doesn't know much about horses but there will be no riding involved, just feeding them and cleaning the stables, keeping an eye on the brood mares. A local man called Maurice comes in twice a day to tend to the stallion and youngstock. Besides that, Cass will do gardening and odd jobs. The clothes she has brought with her are mainly jeans, T-shirts and sweaters, with a few smarter items in case she goes out anywhere.

A thrush is singing outside, pouring its song into the dusk, its repeated phrases. Cass feels several hundred miles away from home instead of just across the Channel, a few hours' journey. This time yesterday she was packing in her own room. Three weeks ago today was the night she woke up suddenly and knew that something had happened.

"You don't mind if I go out with Kelvin on Friday night, do

you?" Robbie asked her on the way back from town.

"Course not, stupid. Where are you going?"

"To a club over at Reading, with Tim and Andy. Tim's brother's group's playing over there." He hesitated. "I mean, you could come too but it's really meant to be a lads' night out."

"Count me out then, definitely. I know what you lot are like when you get laddish," Cass teased. "I'll give Amy a ring. The new Keanu Reeves film's on at the Classic."

"You're welcome." Robbie made a face. He couldn't stand Keanu Reeves. "I'll see you on Saturday then?"

Cass didn't know why he had asked if she minded. Of course not – she didn't own him or feel she had any rights over him. She was grateful for his support during her illness; he had come to visit her even when she had been at her droopiest, bringing her videos and silly puzzles and magazines, cheering her up with jokes and tales from school. It was impossible to feel depressed when Robbie was around. She was surprised by his loyalty – there were plenty of other girls he could have gone out with, and she wouldn't have blamed him. She didn't think their relationship was the clingy sort that meant they had to be together every possible moment. He didn't need to ask for her approval if he wanted to go out with his mates. She wouldn't ask him if she were going somewhere; she would just tell him, knowing that he wouldn't mind at all.

Cass and Amy went to the cinema on Friday night. Afterwards, Cass gave Amy a lift home and went in for coffee, then home to bed. She had slept for some time and had no idea what the time was when she woke suddenly with the certainty that something had happened, something irrevocable.

Perhaps she had been dreaming, but the feeling wouldn't go away. It had happened before, when she had woken up one morning and known for sure that Grandpère Jean-Luc had died in the night.

When Mum had told her the news about Grandpère, she said calmly, "Yes, I know."

Mum stared. "But how do you know?"

Cass said, "I just know."

And she knew now.

When Robbie's mum rang to say that the four boys had been in a car accident and that Robbie had been kept in hospital overnight for observation, the only surprise Cass felt was that it was far less serious than she had imagined. Kelvin, who had been driving, needed only treatment for minor cuts and scratches to his face, and for shock. The others, Tim and Andy, had been kept in hospital too, for concussion.

Cass went with Robbie's mum to collect him. "Trust Kelvin to get away with it," Cass said on the way there, because Kelvin was the sort of person who did. He and Robbie together were like a pair of fourteen-year-olds, nudging each other, having mock fights, convulsing with laughter over ridiculous jokes.

"When those four get together –" Robbie's mum shook her head in affectionate disapproval.

They found Robbie full of elation at having survived. He told them about the accident twice on the way home and then once more for his father's benefit, mapping out the scene with sweeping arm gestures.

"And then this car swerves right across us – I thought I was going right through the windscreen –"

"That young Kelvin," Robbie's dad said. "Driving too fast, if I know anything about it."

And Cass listened, uneasily, because she still didn't know why her premonition suggested something worse than this, something that couldn't be exclaimed over and forgotten. She was sure there was something she didn't know yet.

It was only later that she found out about the other driver.

3. Memorial

During her illness, Cass slept and dozed so much that her dreams began to mingle with her waking thoughts, the books she read and the films she watched. There was one recurring dream, with such intensity of feeling that she remembered it vividly when she woke, recognized it when she slid into it again. In the dream, she is walking along a grassy path towards a cottage. Brambles and thistles clutch at her clothes as she pushes her way through; there is a stagnant, weedy smell and she can see the glint and ripple of water through weeds. As she walks on, the path is so close to the water's edge that mud sucks at her shoes and she feels the ooze of water inside them. Almost hidden by scrubby woodland, the cottage is white-washed, shuttered and slate-roofed, with dark cobwebby gaps where the tiles have slid away. Beside it is a neglected orchard, the trees so gnarled and dark that they appear to crouch, dropping their apples in the long grass to rot. Wasps rise up buzzing as Cass approaches. She is trying to get to the cottage door, but the brambles and thistles tug at her, pulling her back. At one of the upstairs windows a shutter is opened briefly and Cass glimpses a white, frightened face, a child's face, ducking quickly out of sight. The weeds and thorns spring up like a forest, barring her way. Struggling, tearing her hands, forcing her way between the stems until she is trapped and helpless, Cass wakes up to her silent room. The urgency of her mission slips from her mental grasp as she tries to hold on to it. The ending is always the same.

After so long convalescing, Cass likes getting up early, pulling on her work clothes, knowing she has a job to do. She goes downstairs into the iced-water freshness of the April morning: a weak sun over the trees, grass soaked and shining with dew. Even though she rose promptly with her alarm, Maurice is already here, clanking buckets under a tap. Cass met him briefly last night. He must be about sixty, a small, tough man dressed in navy overalls like many French farm-workers, with a creased face and deeply tanned skin. His bicycle leans against the yard fence. Today, he will be staying longer than usual to show Cass what to do.

When each of the horses has been given a full bucket of water, he shows Cass how to measure out scoops of cubes, barley and oats for the morning feeds. There is a chart on the wall showing what each horse is to have. Cass smells the malty dried-grass of the cubes and the floury dust of crushed barley grains as Maurice leans over the bins, scoops and lifts. The oats pour into the feed bowls with a dry hiss. He adds mineral supplements which smell faintly of seaweed and then mixes the feeds in their plastic bowls.

"Leave the stallion to me," he says. "He's a handful, that one. Especially if you're not used to horses."

He gives Cass a doubtful look and she guesses that he is wondering why Monsieur and Madame Martineau have brought a clueless schoolgirl to work here.

He hands her a feed bowl. "Give that to the black mare at the far end. There's a manger in each stable."

The horses know they're going to be fed. They are all looking over their doors, one of them stamping and banging.

Whinnies of expectation greet Cass as she steps out of the feed room. The black mare in the end stable makes a soft whickering sound through her nostrils, follows Cass to the manger at the back and pushes her nose eagerly into the feed, snorting up a fan of oats and dust. Cass strokes her glossy neck. If all the horses are like this, she needn't be afraid. There are four mares – one pregnant, one with a foal – and the stallion, Mistral. Besides the stabled horses, Maurice has told her, there are three yearlings out in one of the fields adjoining the nature reserve.

"Now we fill the hay nets," he says, when all the horses are eating.

"Don't they eat grass?" Cass asks.

A smile twitches at Maurice's thin lips. "When they're out in the fields, yes. They need hay to eat during the night."

"Oh." Cass feels stupid for asking, but Maurice says, "In another few weeks, when the nights aren't so cold and the grass has grown, they'll stay out all the time. They won't need hay then."

She is relieved that he doesn't mind her ignorance, doesn't mind explaining things. He shows her how to tie the hay nets to their rings so that they won't dangle low enough when empty for the horses to tangle their legs in the mesh. By then the horses have finished eating and are ready to be turned out in the paddocks. The mares are placid and docile, making no fuss. With the last, Maurice leads the foal behind its mother and Cass stops by the gate to watch its long-legged skittering as it reaches the freedom of the paddock. Meanwhile, the stallion watches everything that happens, barging at his door and neighing, with a harsh, imperious trumpeting sound. To lead him out, Maurice fetches a stick and a bridle, not a headcollar like the ones the mares wore. Cass stands well back as the dark grey stallion erupts into the yard and plunges across it, snaking his head and neck with such vigour that she's amazed the small man can hold him. The stallion has his own paddock, with a double fence to stop him from reaching the mares. Inside the gate, the moment the bridle is off, he bucks and leaps away, then gallops round his boundary, head up, tail streaming, looking across at the mares and sending out his trumpeting whinny.

Maurice shakes his head as he bolts the gate. "Needs a firm hand, that one."

Cass admires the stallion's arrogance and beauty but prefers the gentle mares. She is glad she won't be the one providing the firm hand. She dreads going into Mistral's stable, although she will have to at some point. Maurice won't always be around when the stallion needs feeding or watering.

Oncle Gérard comes down during the morning and looks at all the horses, commenting to Maurice on their condition. By lunchtime the stables are all cleaned out, with fresh beds of shavings ready for the horses when they come in later. Maurice cycles off, promising to come back at six. Upstairs in her flat Cass makes herself a snack lunch and then decides to walk to the village, two kilometres away. There are gardening jobs for her to do this afternoon but she decides to adopt the French custom of taking a leisurely lunch-break. If she waits in the village until two, she can buy bread at the *boulangerie* and go to the small supermarket she noticed yesterday as she drove through.

Leaving the stud farm by the side gate, she passes the

entrance to the bird reserve. There is a big board illustrating some of the birds likely to be seen here – waders, ducks, birds of prey – and a map showing where the trails are, the hide and the best viewing points. Tomorrow she will walk round, Cass decides, although she hasn't got binoculars. Dad would like it here. He loves birdwatching, sitting for hours in a freezing hide with his flask and his sandwiches and his telescope, chatting to fellow enthusiasts about green sandpipers and red-backed shrikes. Occasionally, on holidays, Cass has accompanied him. Once Robbie went with Dad, although he got bored as soon as he realized that rarities didn't queue up in front of the telescope to be admired, and wanted to do something more exciting.

Coming out from the scrubby woodland that circles the reserve, Cass sees the village of St Privat in its slight dip, behind a row of grey-blue poplars. The church spire dominates the cluster of grey buildings. A dog barks at Cass as she passes a farmyard but when she enters the village the whole place looks silent, shut up. Several of the buildings fronting the street have closed shutters and even the café-bar doesn't seem open; the *boulangerie/pâtisserie* has a glorious display of Easter *tartes* and gateaux but its door shows a *Fermé* sign. There is no pavement and the road is dusty in the midday warmth. Cass looks at her watch. Twenty to two – the supermarket won't open for another twenty minutes.

In front of the church, which is large and imposing for such a small village, there is a fountain and a war memorial. *Morts pour la France* – the memorial is identical in design to those Cass has seen in countless other towns and villages, with its spray of laurel in relief. Except that this one has names from her own family on it. She goes closer to read them. Two wars, two lists of names. The First World War claimed twenty-five lives from this small settlement, the Second fewer. The name Dupasquier appears in both lists: Louis and Armand, in the first batch, Félix in the second, with the date 1940. Cass knows that Félix Dupasquier is – or would have been – her great-uncle, Tante Eugénie's brother. If Félix hadn't died, he would have inherited Le Clos d'If, rather than Eugénie. Tante Eugénie inherited the house and farm just after she married Oncle Gérard and changed her name to Martineau. Claude Dupasquier, her father, shot himself shortly before the end of the war, although Cass has no idea why: perhaps from grief for the death of Félix, his only son. Tante Eugénie has no children, and Cass's dad has sometimes speculated on what will happen to the house and farm after she dies. It is a subject that Cass's mother refuses to discuss.

Three Dupasquiers on one memorial. The family suffered badly in the two wars. But Cass can see for herself that other families did too – whole clutches of Hoques, Lebruns, Martins.

The village is so quiet in the dusty sunshine that it is almost eerie. Standing by the memorial, Cass feels suddenly exhausted. Perhaps she should have rested after lunch instead of setting out on a walk; she is supposed to mow all the lawns this afternoon and should have conserved her strength. The silence of the village is so intense that it invades her head with heaviness. She sits down on a stone bench, resisting the urge to lie full-length and sleep. Someone is watching her, an instinct warns: she is suddenly alert, her skin prickling. The feeling makes her self-conscious of her movements, all desire to sleep gone. But there is no one around; not even the twitching of a curtain suggests a curious onlooker.

4. Reserve

The English visitors arrive that afternoon: a youngish couple called Jilly and Keith Wadebridge, with two children. Meeting Jilly halfway upstairs with a box loaded with paté, Chardonnay and cheeses, Cass introduces herself. Jilly invites her in for tea later, which Cass takes as a friendly gesture until she realizes that Jilly's motive is to pump her for information about where to go locally to keep the children amused. Cass can only suggest, rather obviously, the beaches. The children, Sophie and Charles, are noisy and demanding, already bored, complaining that there's no video and that EuroDisney is too far away, pulling at their mother's arm when she tries to talk to Cass. Jilly is about thirty with a jaded, blonde prettiness, and looks rather wearied by the children; she is disappointed that Cass won't be able to provide pony rides. Her husband Keith has settled into an armchair with a bottle of wine and apparently intends to stay there while Jilly unpacks the groceries and prepares a meal.

"It's going to be a bit quiet for them here," Jilly remarks, looking out of the window.

"That's why we chose it," Keith reminds her. "Surely they can find things to do around the farm?" He looks at Cass hopefully, and she hopes they're not proposing to use her as childminder. Sophie and Charles are far too brattish for her taste.

"Aren't you lonely, out here in the middle of nowhere?" Jilly asks Cass. "Haven't you got a boyfriend or anything?"

"Yes, I have," Cass says.

Jilly tilts her head as if she wants to hear more. Why is it, Cass wonders, that couples always seem to want everyone else to get paired off as well? She isn't a pair. She's herself. And she doesn't know why she answered "Yes" to Jilly's question. She isn't sure that Robbie *is* her boyfriend.

"A French boyfriend?" Jilly lifts her eyebrows suggestively.

"No. English. At home in England."

"Not much use to you here, then," Keith says.

Uncomfortably, she thinks of the postcard that arrived this morning at the main house with *Je t'aime* on it again, written in French for anyone to read. She will have to write back, even if it's just a postcard, but she has no idea what to say. *Je t'aime* is a statement, a declaration, calling for a response of some kind. She can't match it but it doesn't seem right just to ignore it.

Tante Eugénie is disappointed when Cass refuses to go to Mass next day.

"Not on Easter Sunday?" Her plucked eyebrows rise above blue powdered lids. "Not even today?"

Cass shakes her head. As she doesn't go to church regularly, it would be hypocritical to go today just because it's Easter. "I never do."

Tante Eugénie shakes her head, mouth primly tight. "Such pity. Your mother doesn't go any more, either?"

"Not every Sunday. She might go today, though."

Cass knows that if her mother does go, it will be in the face of Dad's scepticism. "Going for your dose of guilt and incense?" he will say, settling down comfortably with a cup of coffee and *The Observer*.

At Le Clos d'If, Sundays are organized around church attendance. Cass will do morning and evening stables but will have the rest of the day free, apart from the obligatory lunch at the house. Maurice comes as usual in the morning but leaves on his bicycle in good time to go home and change. Tante Eugénie, it appears, goes to both morning and evening Mass. Cass suspects that Oncle Gérard is less devout than his wife but goes for the sake of appearance and tradition. She sees him backing his old black Citroën out of the garage where it has stayed locked up for most of the week.

"Could you give me a lift down to the village when you go?" she asks him, thinking of using her free time to walk back through the bird reserve.

Oncle Gérard agrees, but when Tante Eugénie comes down from the house, dressed for church in a suit of sombre dark blue, Cass can tell that she isn't pleased. Evidently, she doesn't approve of the churchward journey being used as a convenient means of transport. She sits in the passenger seat clutching her handbag and missal. Perhaps she is composing herself into a suitable frame of mind for Easter Sunday Mass as she says nothing at all during the short drive, dismissing Cass outside the church: "Lunch is at one o'clock. Please don't be late. We'll see you at the house."

Cass feels curious eyes on her as she gets out of the back seat of the Citroën. She is identifiable now that she has been seen with her great-aunt and uncle, no longer a wandering tourist who has strayed into the village. The church bell's single note sounds out into the clear air, a tone that to Cass is peculiarly French. On the church steps there stands a tall man, of similar age to the Martineaus, with iron-grey hair rushed sleekly back from a long, beaky-nosed face. He is apparently waiting for someone, but as Tante Eugénie and Oncle Gérard mount the steps he nods curtly, turning his back on them as if to avoid speaking. Or has Cass imagined it? People are drifting towards the church, so many that Cass wonders where they were all hiding yesterday. The church-goers are mainly middle-aged and elderly, with only a few younger people and children. They go up the steps and disappear into the shadowy, candlelit interior. The beaky-nosed man is joined by a couple in their forties and they all go in last. Cass imagines for herself the smell of incense inside, the polished wood and the light through stained-glass, the devout silence.

If she were going to church and could pray, she would pray for the man called David Thwaite who is lying in an intensive care ward in Reading, the victim of Kelvin's Friday night recklessness. A young man, twenty-seven, with two small children. Or for his wife, who doesn't know yet whether she will be a widow.

But Cass can't pray. Praying isn't something you can turn to only in times of stress, inventing a faith that isn't present in everyday life, as if God's sitting there at the end of a Samaritan phone line. And if God exists, why did he let the accident happen at all?

Cass enters the reserve car-parking area close to the village, where there is the same illustrated map-board that she has seen at the other entrance, nearer the stables. The soft ground is rutted by tyres but there are no vehicles parked here. The paths round the reserve are indicated by coloured notches in wooden posts. Wishing Dad were here to lend her his binoculars and identify the various birds, Cass sets off along a path between sallows and flag irises. Already she can hear one bird she recognizes: a chiff-chaff, spring arrival, with its jaunty repeated call. She looks up into the sallows but can't see where the bird is perched. She doesn't know its French name because all her birdwatching has been done with her father. The expanse of water opens up to her left. Looking across, she can see various ducks, some in a swimming flotilla, some resting on the grass on the far side, but she can't identify them at this range. Farther along, beyond a thicker clump of scrubby trees, she can see the slatted wood and hinged flaps of a birdwatching hide. The path leads on round, so close to the lake's edge that water seeps across the path. Cass jumps the puddles but can't avoid splashing mud up her jeans; her trainers aren't watertight and she can feel dampness around her toes. The path is overgrown, evidently not as well-used as she had imagined.

She is in her dream.

It seems so inevitable that she isn't frightened at first, only curious. She continues walking as if she has no choice. The path veers abruptly round an unexpected inlet. To the right, away from the path, is a small copse of poplars; to the left, the widening grassy shore and the wooden hide. Cass's eyes are drawn to the trees. Through the mist of budding leaves, she glimpses the cottage, without surprise. It is more derelict than in her dream – the door boarded up, shutters hanging off, part of the roof completely caved in – but she knows it is the same building. The orchard surrounding it must have been left untended for years. The bent, gnarled apple trees are swamped for half their height in bramble, pale pink blossom rising like foam above the encroaching tangle. The path Cass has been following keeps to the water's edge; there is no track, not even an overgrown one, leading to the cottage door. Leaving the path, she wades through the undergrowth, disentangling herself from the clutch of brambles. She doesn't know why she has to reach the cottage, but the clarity and urgency of her dream return to her and she looks up, remembering the fearful, white-faced child at the window. There is no face there now. Of course not – the cottage doesn't look as if anyone's been near it for years. The brickwork is crumbling away from the door-frame, and inside Cass sees bare concrete, with nettles and ground-elder thrusting up through gaps. The boards over the door are held on loosely by rusting nails. Cass pulls at one, feels it yield and knows that she could easily break in if she wanted to. She would prefer the way to be securely barred with rails and barbed wire, taking away any choice.

She stands there, hesitating. Her instincts are at war with each other. Curiosity tells her to pull off the boards and go in; it's only a derelict cottage. A deeper, stronger instinct tells her to run, to leave the place alone. Fear creeps up her neck, along her arms, into her throat, from a dark hollow place somewhere in her chest. A blackbird nearby gives its busy, clacking alarm call. Cass turns, barely controlling her panic as she thrashes her way back to the path. It doesn't matter that it's a calm spring day with the sunlight glancing off the water and the ducks preening themselves, unconcerned. With the odd certainty that has proved reliable before, she knows that something terrible has happened here.

* * *

Back in her flat, she changes for Sunday lunch. After registering Tante Eugénie's shocked glance at her leggings and baggy sweater on Friday night, she knows better than to appear casually dressed for today's meal. She has already upset her great-aunt by not attending church and she is willing to concede to her on dress policy. Eating is taken seriously, a focal point in the day.

She changes into a long buttoned skirt and a plain black jumper, puts on tights and shoes and goes to the mirror to brush her hair loose. Cécile's face looks back at her from the mirror, a pale face between sweeps of hair. A demure French girl dressed neatly for visiting relatives on Sunday. Cass is more tomboyish, with her hair pulled back in a plait or ponytail and her workmanlike clothes and boots. As Cécile her eyes look larger, more mysterious, guarding their secrets. What does she know? She is puzzled by the dream and the different reality of the cottage, the strange prickly atmosphere of both. Why has she seen it so vividly? It is as if the dream has pulled her here, the familiar tug of France bringing her not just to Normandy but to this specific place: this house, this lake, this tumbledown cottage. Her own face is a stranger's, telling her nothing. She frowns at herself, puts on silver stud earrings and a chain necklace, and goes over to the house.

Sunday lunch is formal, served in the high-ceilinged dining room with its dark furniture and high-backed chairs and gilt-framed oil paintings. Cass knows it well from previous visits and it always reminds her of a rather staid, old-fashioned restaurant, where people talk in hushed voices and waiters over respectfully. Nothing has changed since Cass's earliest visits – the gold-rimmed china is exactly as she remembers and the same crystal decanter sits on the sideboard – and she has the odd feeling that time has stood still, having to remind herself that she's seventeen now, not a little girl dressed up in her best frock and patent shoes for the visit. The food will be served, as usual, by Madame Gautier, the Martineaus' cook/housekeeper, who nods and smiles at Cass in recognition as she enters but afterwards pours the drinks in silence. The *buffet* is stacked ready with dessert dishes and coffee cups. The table is covered with a lace-edged cloth and set with heavy French cutlery and wineglasses, and has a centrepiece of Easter daffodils and primroses. Tante Eugénie has taken off the navy jacket she wore for church. Her hair is swept back from her forehead and her lipstick reapplied. She smiles at Cass, evidently approving of her neat attire, and offers her an aperitif. Not used to drinking at lunchtime, Cass refuses. There is a carafe of *vin rouge* on the table, and wine with the meal will be enough for her to cope with.

"We are having a traditional local menu today, for your first Sunday lunch with us," Tante Eugénie explains. She is more expansive now, entering into her hostess role, her church-going solemnity put aside until the evening.

Madame Gautier serves fish soup with golden croutons and cream, lamb in a piquant sauce with beans and gratin potatoes. During the meal, Oncle Gérard talks about the horses, his recent purchase of the young stallion Mistral and his breeding plans. Tante Eugénie isn't interested in the horses at all; she asks Cass a lot of questions about her mother. "So Thérèse is well, you say? Will she be coming to visit this year? Is she still enjoying her job? Thinking of early retirement yet?"

Madame Gautier refills the bread basket and brings in cheeses. The conversation moves on to Cass herself. "Have you thought of studying in France instead of going back to your English school? Taking the International Baccalauréat, perhaps? A career in Paris? You ought to take advantage of being bilingual, Cécile, my dear. Many young people would envy you that."

"Maybe she will take up a career with horses," Oncle Gérard says, only half-serious.

Cass laughs. "Become a champion jockey? I'd need to learn to ride first." But she can't answer Tante Eugénie's more serious questions. She doesn't know what she wants to do. It's her life, but she can't get round to considering it yet.

Dessert is brought in, a choice: an Easter *tarte* like the ones in the *pâtisserie* window, decorated with confectionery eggs and flowers, or *Tarte Tatin*, a pastry case containing thin slices of apple, overlapping, browned and caramelized with baking. To follow, there is strong coffee and Calvados. The powerful scent of pure apple fills Cass's senses as she lifts her liqueur glass, calling to mind orchards in late summer, baskets loaded with ripe fruit, wasps. Her dream.

The food, the wine and the Calvados are combining to make her relax for the first time in the company of her great-uncle and aunt. She sits back in her chair, fingers cradling the smooth glass and tilting the amber liquid.

"I walked through the reserve today," she remarks.

"Oh, yes." Oncle Gérard passes chocolates in a china dish. "Someone saw a little egret there the other day. Migrating."

"I didn't see many birds," Cass says, "but I wondered about the derelict cottage in there, near the lake. What was it? How long has it been empty?"

Her question is left hanging in the air for a moment. Tante Eugénie and Oncle Gérard don't look at each other or at Cass but there is a sudden awkwardness, a tension, like a wire strung out between them, tingling to hidden vibrations. Tante Eugénie stirs her coffee and raises the cup, her lips pursed ready to drink.

"It used to be a gamekeeper's cottage, when the lake was used for shooting," Oncle Gérard says. "There's been no use for it since."

"Have some more coffee, Cécile." Tante Eugénie busies herself with the pot and the cream jug. "I'm not sure it's a good idea for you to wander round that reserve on your own. Anyone might go in there. Tourists, even poachers, at quiet times."

"Oh, I don't think there's any need for—" Oncle Gérard begins, but is silenced by a look from his wife.

Cass can't imagine meeting anyone dangerous by the lake or the birdwatching hide. She isn't sure she wants to go back there anyway after her near-panic, not to the cottage at any rate, but she is still curious. It occurs to her that maybe the cottage was where her great-grandfather shot himself; that could explain why the subject isn't a welcome one for discussion. She has always assumed that he did it in the house, although it seems odd now that she has never really thought about it. Wouldn't Tante Eugénie have preferred to move away instead of living in this sombre house? There must be memories everywhere, even without Cass to put her foot in it by asking tactless questions. In spite of today's Easter flowers, the lavish food and the elegant style, Le Clos d'If is a sad, secretive place, guarding its sorrows.

5. Yearlings

One of the mares, Mélodie, is due to foal within the next week. Maurice and Cass prepare the big foaling box, disinfecting the wall and floor and then, when it's dry, laying a thick bed of straw, well banked-up at the sides. There is a hatch from the harness-room next door so that the groom (Maurice? herself?) can keep watch without having to stand out in the yard all night.

Cass is getting used to the horses. Especially she likes the docile mares, the warm smell of them, their heavy grace, the calm alertness of their brown eyes. In the evenings when work is finished she likes to walk along the row of stables to look at each horse in turn, some lying down, others eating their hay with a steady rhythmic sound that fills her with deep contentment. Although she is still wary of the stallion she has learned to enter his stable without signalling too obviously that she is afraid.

"Be assertive," Maurice has told her. "Don't creep in like a frightened mouse. Walk straight in as if you mean it."

Cass has learned to fool herself, even if not the horse, taking a deep breath as she slides the bolt back and then marching in with the feed or the water-bucket. The stallion is young and unpredictable, given to lashing out with a hind hoof if an insect annoys him or plunging round his stable if his food doesn't arrive quickly enough. He doesn't mean any harm, Maurice says: he isn't vicious, just *méchant*. He uses the word in its affectionate sense, meaning naughty or playful. Cass isn't sure she can tell the difference, not yet.

Midweek, she and Maurice walk up the lane to move the yearlings to another paddock. There is little grass in the paddock they have occupied over the winter and they have trodden the gateway and the area around the trough into a hoof-marked morass. Moving them out will give the grass a chance to grow, Maurice says; it is important to give each field a rest. Their new paddock is closer to the stables, a short distance along the lane.

"They haven't been handled enough, these youngsters," Maurice warns Cass. "They're half-wild. You'll have to keep a tight grip."

There are three of them, young thoroughbreds. They look like overgrown foals, with half-grown tufty tails and babyish eyes that show the whites. In spite of what Maurice has said, they come willingly enough for a bucket of oats and he puts a headcollar on each one in turn. He is going to lead two, Cass the remaining one, a light bay colt. The yearlings are nervous at leaving their field and there is a mêlée in the gateway before Cass and Maurice succeed in getting them out on to the lane and closing the gate behind them.

Cass's colt is stronger than she imagined. Not used to being led, it throws up its head and tugs at the rope, skittering sideways. Maurice glances round to see how she is coping but has his hands full with the other two. They are making erratic progress along the tree-bordered lane when a whirring of wings and cracking of twigs sounds abruptly from the hedge behind Cass, startling both her and the colt. He pulls back, then rears on his hind legs, and for an instant his hooves flail in front of Cass's face. Determined not to let go, she hangs on to the rope and is jerked forward as the yearling barges forward into the other two.

"Whoa! Whoa!" she gasps.

Suddenly there are horses all over the road, hooves skidding, ropes straining, and in the confusion Cass sees Maurice knocked to the ground among trampling hooves. Winded, he hangs on to the ropes. The yearlings drag him along in their panic and then stop, their eyes rolling; they are frightened by the dead weight and the commotion.

"Maurice! *Maurice!* Are you all right?" Cass tries to lead her reluctant colt towards him. She is sure he has been kicked, if not trodden on.

Maurice shakes his head slowly and tries to rise, then clutches at his chest.

"It hurts – here –"

Cass looks around wildly. There's no one to help and she is sure that Maurice is having a heart attack. What are the symptoms? What should be done? She is terrified of doing the wrong thing.

"Lie down, and stay there. Give me the ropes." She takes the leads from him and he lies down on the dusty tarmac. His face is pale, frightened. Now she is holding all three yearlings. What next? She can't manage all three and she can't let them loose – they might gallop out on to the road, cause another accident.

"Lead one. The others will follow," Maurice says, with a painful effort. He is lying on his back, one leg bent up, both hands held to his throat. "Then phone from the stables. I'll be all right."

Cass doubts it. She unclips two of the ropes, keeping hold

of the light bay colt she started with and hoping there are no more birds to make it career off. She glances back at Maurice, afraid he will be dead by the time she gets back. The colt jogs and frets, refusing to be calmed, and the other two surge alongside so that Cass can't avoid being shoved and jolted. She reaches the open gateway, steers the yearling inside, and mercifully the other two follow, tempted by the lush grass. She bolts the gate and runs back to the stableyard as fast as she can. The yard is deserted; the Wadebridges' green Mondeo is gone from its parking place, or she would have asked one of them to drive back and wait with Maurice. From the phone in the harness-room she calls emergency services and explains what has happened, and where. Then she rings the house to tell Oncle Gérard, grabs a bottle of mineral water from the shelf for Maurice and runs back down the lane.

It's all her fault! The words ring in her head in time with her running feet. *My fault, my fault.* If she weren't so useless with nervous horses, so inexperienced, she wouldn't have let her colt barge forward and Maurice wouldn't have been knocked over. Because of her, Maurice might die of a heart attack. She thinks of him lying alone in the road, dying. When she rounds the corner she sees him there on the ground in his blue overalls like a bundle dropped off the back of a lorry, a Guy Fawkes doll.

"Maurice?" she calls, hardly daring to approach. How long will the ambulance take to get here? But if he is dead, it won't matter how long.

And then Maurice raises a hand. As she goes nearer his blue eyes look up at her and he gives a painful smile.

"You were quick. It's my ribs, I think."

Cass crouches down beside him and offers him the water. He shakes his head. She realizes that he is right not to move, if he thinks his ribs are broken. To her relief, his colour has returned. Not a heart attack after all.

"I'm sorry," she says inadequately.

Maurice's hand waves again. "Not your fault. Those colts left to run half-wild – asking for trouble."

Cass looks up. Oncle Gérard is walking along the lane, as quickly as he can manage with his stiff gait. The ambulance will be here soon. Someone else will take control.

When the ambulance has taken Maurice away, Cass walks slowly back to the stables. She feels utterly drained – the running, and the tension, have proved to her how unfit she still is after her illness. Waves of dizziness crash through her head and she climbs the stairs to her flat. The morning stablework is all finished but she will have to do the evening jobs by herself. She thinks of the stallion out in the paddock and wonders how she is going to get him back to his stable. If she can't handle a harmless yearling, how is she going to manage Mistral? But she is too tired to worry now. She lies down on her bed, fully-dressed, and waits for the room to stop revolving.

Images of the other, more horrific accident float into her head. She wasn't there to see it – thankfully – but she has seen the photographs in the local paper and has imagined it for herself, countless times over, until it is there in her head, lodged firmly, replaying itself in slow motion whenever she lets it. Kelvin's Escort rounding a bend, too fast, cutting across the middle of the road. The other driver hauling at the wheel as he swerves. The violent clash of metal on metal as the two cars collide, the Granada veering off the road, turning over, rolling down the bank. Robbie and his friends staggering out of the Escort, staring at each other's bloodied faces, taking stock of the damage. And in the Granada, trapped upside down, the other driver, who isn't moving at all.

Robbie's mum on the phone, three days later: "Aren't you coming round to see him? He wants you."

Her own voice, awkward. "No. Not today."

"When, then?" Robbie's mum sounded impatient. "After all he did for you when you were ill. I'd have thought you could make a bit of an effort. I'd have thought you owed it to him."

"I expect you're right," Cass said, although she finds the situation too complex to be able to say with any certainty who owes what, or to whom.

"It's Kelvin you ought to blame, if you want to blame someone," Robbie's mum said. "It wasn't Robbie's fault. He wasn't the one driving."

Cass doesn't think it's as simple as that. The accident could have happened at any time. Four boys out for the night, drinking, having a laugh – it's not the first time. They are all responsible. Maybe she is, too. She has accepted lifts from Kelvin – though not so often now that she has her own car – and has seen how he drives: flashy, aggressive, jumping the lights, racing the engine, disregarding speed limits as if they apply only to lesser mortals. Relieved to get out of the car safely, she has said nothing. What she should have said is: "Kelvin, you're a bloody idiot. Do you want to kill someone?"

Now he nearly has.

Robbie could have been killed, too. Robbie wasn't driving, but he has never criticized either. He just laughs, sitting in the passenger seat with a can of lager, turning up the stereo. Enjoying the speed and the power. Lads having a good time.

In the evening Oncle Gérard comes down to the stables to bring in the stallion and look at the pregnant mare.

"I wasn't sure whether you could cope with Mistral on your own," he explains.

Cass goes with him to open the gate. The stallion is suspicious, sensing a change in the routine. Instead of coming quietly as he does for Maurice, he ducks away from the headcollar and trots fast across the paddock, tail streaming. It takes five attempts and a refill of oats before he is caught. Oncle Gérard puffs and lurches as the stallion dashes round him in mad circles, refusing to walk sensibly. At last they reach Mistral's stable and Cass shuts the door gratefully. Oncle Gérard wipes his face with a big handkerchief.

"We're going to have to get someone else," he says. "Maurice's wife rang when they got back from hospital. His ribs are cracked and he won't be back at work for a few weeks. We can't manage on our own. And this horse needs a firm hand."

"Is there anyone?" Cass asks.

"I'll have to give it some thought. Phone around," Oncle Gérard says.

Later, when she has finished feeding and watering the horses, Cass goes up to the house to return the key of the outhouse where the lawnmower is kept. The front door is ajar and she goes into the entrance hall. Wood-panelled and

shadowy, with thin strips of maroon carpet between the doors
it always gives her the feeling of entering a chapel, a feeling
enhanced by the presence of another Madonna, alabaster, in a
recessed alcove lit by a single candle. The figurine's eyes are
downcast and one graceful hand is raised to its cheek, giving
the appearance of deep sorrow. Cass has seen Tante Eugénie
pause and cross herself each time she passes it. Cass is
wearing trainers but all the same her footsteps sound loud in
the shadowy hush, as if she has been too brash and noisy in
her entrance, although no one comes to see what she wants.

She hesitates, wondering whether to find Madame Gautier
Then, from the sitting-room, she hears her great-aunt's and
uncle's voices and she realizes that they're arguing.

"If you can think of anyone better than Duclos, then tell
me!"

"I don't want him here." Tante Eugénie, her voice quiet,
firm.

"It's not a matter of what you want. We'll be lucky if he
agrees. But he needs work at the moment, so I hear. Times are
difficult. I'll go over and see him tomorrow."

"Surely it's not necessary. Cécile can manage."

"Of course she can't! Not in the stud season. She's a good
girl but she knows next to nothing about horses. She can't
manage that stallion – I could barely hang on to him myself
We don't want another accident. And besides we've got the
mare due to foal and one still to be covered. How can she cope
with that on her own? And what about her day off on Fridays?
We can't expect her to work seven days a week."

"All right," Tante Eugénie concedes, "but I don't want
Pascal Duclos here and I can't imagine him agreeing. His

grandfather – Can't you find someone else? Try an advertisement or an agency?"

A sarcastic huff from Oncle Gérard. "What, for tomorrow?"

There is a silence. Cass imagines them glaring at each other. She would like to ask if they have heard any more about Maurice, but doesn't want them to know she has overheard their argument. She dithers uncertainly in the entrance hall, decides to leave the key on the table and lets herself out.

6. Nowhere

In the morning Cass gets up at her usual time and goes down to the yard. It feels quiet without Maurice, although there is the usual excited stir of neighing and banging when she appears. She goes about her usual duties, watering, feeding, taking the mares out to graze. Oncle Gérard doesn't appear and the stallion is still caged up in his stable, pawing at the floor, neighing in his loud indignant voice.

Cass decides that she will have to take him out herself. Remembering that Maurice always puts a bridle on him and carries a stick, she fetches them from the harness-room and stands outside the stable for a few moments, trying to convince herself that in five minutes' time the stallion will be safely in his paddock. He is snatching at the remnants of his hay, not really eating, just bored and impatient. Cass knows that the worst thing she can do is let him know she is afraid.

She goes into the stable and approaches him, patting his shoulder. He twitches his skin irritably but does nothing drastic.

"There's a good lad." She doesn't sound nervous but she bets Mistral knows better. Holding out a handful of cubes, she manages to slip the bit into his mouth while he's eating, and fastens the buckles of the bridle.

"Good boy!"

Somehow it's not the right way to speak to the stallion, as if he's a pet dog, and anyway she's talking to calm herself, no him. She opens the stable door and grasps the lead rein firmly in one hand, the stick in the other. Mistral clatters out, trying to make a dash for the mares' paddock; if she lets him go, out in the yard she will never catch him again. The distance between her and the gate stretches out like a marathon. Deliberately keeping her pace slow and regular, she holds the stick at the ready in case the stallion tries to swing round and face her. She manages to hold him back until they reach the gateway, where he turns towards her and strikes out with a front foot.

"No, you don't!"

She is ready with her stick, smacking him across the chest. Stepping aside, she slips the bridle off and watches as he bucks and leaps, then careers off on his regular tour of the boundary. She's done it! It feels like passing a major test. This evening she will have to do it again, but that's hours away. And he didn't play her up as much as he did Oncle Gérard.

Back in the yard she finds her great-uncle gazing in dismay at the empty stable, as if he thinks the stallion has escaped. Seeing the bridle and stick Cass is holding, he says, "Oh, you've managed. I was just coming to put him out myself." He sounds relieved that he won't have to.

"He wasn't too bad," Cass says.

"Well done. Now let's have a look at that mare. I've found someone to take over from Maurice, by the way, starting tomorrow. Pascal Duclos, a local chap."

So he's having his own way, Cass thinks. She wonders why Tante Eugénie doesn't want this Duclos person around.

"Who is he?" she asks.

"He used to work on a stud owned by a friend of mine, a few years back," Oncle Gérard says. "He's a reliable worker and good with the horses. That's our main problem solved, eh? So you won't be left all on your own."

After lunch, Cass goes to Maurice's house to see how he is, and to return his cycle. He lives in a small house on the village square. His wife, Madame Lepin, opens the door and takes Cass through to a main room dominated by an oak table and sideboard. Maurice is propped up uncomfortably on a reclining garden chair by the terrace window. He already has a visitor – an elderly man in a dark jacket, who is drinking beer.

"*Salut*, Cass. It's nice of you to come," Maurice says.

Cass gives him the red tulips she has bought at the supermarket.

"My wife, Yvonne," Maurice says. "And this is Monsieur Duclos."

Duclos? Cass registers the name. Probably just a coincidence. It's a common enough surname.

"Gaston," Maurice says to the visitor, "this is Cass, Madame Martineau's great-niece. My saviour yesterday."

Cass thinks this is generous of him: he could justifiably have said, "Cass, who let her horse barge into me and knock me over." But neither Maurice nor his wife appears to bear her any grudge. Monsieur Duclos stands to acknowledge Cass and she recognizes the tall bearing, beaky nose and iron-grey hair of the man she saw on the church steps on Sunday, the man who turned aside to avoid speaking to the Martineaus. Doubtful, she takes the hand he proffers. He shakes her hand in a strong grip and says, "You're working with the horses, I hear. Dangerous creatures, it seems." His eyes are watery blue, filmy.

"Not usually," Cass says.

"You'll be meeting Gaston's grandson, so he's just been telling me," Maurice says. "Pascal's going to help out with the horses."

"Yes, Oncle Gérard told me about it this morning," Cass says.

Not a coincidence, then, after all.

Gaston Duclos does not comment. He picks up his beer glass and drains it. Cass notices that his fingers are stained saffron-yellow by nicotine.

"Does your grandson live in the village?" she asks him.

"No, in Villeneuve." He does not seem inclined to talk about his grandson. He stands and straightens his lapels. "Well, I must go and weed my vegetables. Look after yourself, Maurice. Goodbye, Yvonne, Cass."

Madame Lepin goes to the door with him. Cass watches him go, thinking of his evasive gesture on the church steps, and the remark Tante Eugénie began to make last night about Pascal's grandfather.

"Doesn't Monsieur Duclos like my aunt and uncle?" she asks Maurice.

He is bent over the bunch of tulips, unwrapping the cellophane. "Not much. It goes back a long way. So you've noticed that, have you?"

Maurice's wife returns to the room and sits on one of the dining chairs. She is a stocky woman, with a broad face and hair pinned flatly against her head. "That," she remarks. "It goes back to the war."

"To the war! But that was more than fifty years ago!" Cass exclaims.

"People have long memories in a small place like this," Maurice says. "There aren't enough young people here to make us forget, that's our trouble. All the young folk go away. There's no life for them in a village like this, no work."

His eyes flicker towards a framed photograph on the sideboard, of a smiling young woman with two infant children.

"Your daughter?" Cass prompts.

"Yes. Simone. She lives in Cherbourg now. Her husband works for Brittany ferries. So did she, until she had the children."

Cass is still thinking about Monsieur Duclos and his ancient grievance. "What happened then, in the war? Did Monsieur Duclos argue with my aunt and uncle about something?"

"With your aunt. Your uncle wasn't living here then." Madame Lepin reaches across to take the tulips from Maurice and starts rummaging in one of the sideboard cupboards for a vase. Maurice darts a look at her, but she is moving china plates and dishes from the depths of the cupboard, and doesn't notice.

"Why did they argue?" Cass persists.

"Because he and your aunt were engaged to be married." Madame Lepin straightens up, holding a fluted green vase.

"And then my uncle came along and she broke it off?" Cass guesses.

Madame Lepin hesitates. Maurice shifts his feet on the canvas recliner and says, "Something like that, yes. Yvonne, aren't you going to offer Cass something to drink?"

Leaving the village, Cass finds herself unthinkingly turning in at the reserve entrance. She hadn't intended to come this way and hasn't really got time for a detour; she is supposed to weed her aunt's herbaceous borders this afternoon and then tidy the harness-room before fetching the horses in and settling them for the night. But her feet want to go that way. Something is pulling her back to the lakeside and the deserted cottage. Curiosity overcomes fear as she treads the muddy path so familiar from her dreams. There are no cars in the parking area to indicate visitors; no birdwatchers' telescopes project from the waterside, and the flap of the wooden hide is closed. A willow-warbler's descending call drifts across the lake. The midday warmth hangs over the water's surface, barely a ripple disturbing the trees' reflections. Cass is so certain of her solitude that her heart leaps with alarm when she hears a rustling in the undergrowth beside the path and comes face to face with a child, a small girl of about seven or eight. The girl stares back at Cass, her eyes big and frightened in a thin face. She is dark-haired, dressed shabbily in a gingham blouse and a droopy skirt, her legs thin above ankle socks and bar shoes.

Cass's first thought is that the girl must have wandered away from a birdwatching parent.

"Are you lost? Where have you come from?" she asks, gently.

The child stares at her, wary, her mouth quivering on the verge of speaking.

"Where do you live?" Cass asks again.

"Nowhere." It is barely a whisper. Then, more loudly, as if wanting to establish a truth, the girl repeats, "Nowhere. I don't live anywhere."

Her dark eyes dart wildly from side to side as if she expects Cass to grab or hurt her. Then, abruptly, she is gone, dashing between the shrubby trees in a flurry of limbs, heading towards the cottage.

"Wait!"

Cass plunges after her. The cottage isn't a safe place for a child to play in; the brickwork is crumbling, the stairs might give way. Intent on pushing her way through the clutching undergrowth, Cass has lost sight of the girl, can't hear so much as a snapping twig to indicate where she has gone. At the cottage Cass stops and looks around, baffled. The door is still boarded up. Looking through the gap in the bricks she sees the bare concrete inside, the rotting wooden stairs, the nettles and elder.

"Hello! Are you in there?" she calls.

Her voice echoes in the empty shell of the house and bounces back at her. Cass looks over her shoulder, edgily, to see if anyone has followed her from the lake. The strange atmosphere of the place is reaching her again. Shivers of fear crawl over her skin and tickle the back of her neck.

She is determined not to panic this time. She walks away slowly, fighting the urge to run. It is like handling the stallion - handling her own fear, telling herself there is nothing to be afraid of. Just an old gamekeeper's cottage and a child from the village playing games.

But the girl wasn't playing games, Cass knows that. The child's thin, frightened face is the one she has seen in her dreams. It is the face she has seen at the upstairs window of the cottage.

* * *

In the middle of the night Cass wakes abruptly, staring at the curtained window with the shock of not knowing where she is. She hasn't been dreaming but her cottage dream is vividly with her, and the face of the nowhere girl. Puzzle-pieces dance in her head, teasing, defying her attempts to find sense and meaning. The derelict cottage, the girl; her great-grandfather's suicide; the wartime feud between Monsieur Duclos and Tante Eugénie: there is something here to discover, if only she knew how. And people know, people could tell her, but they won't. Perhaps everyone knows? There are secrets everywhere: in the house, in the village, in the nature reserve. How can she find out?

She slides out of bed and pushes back the curtain, looking out. There is a faint wind, stirring the trees; cloud fragments glide over a transparent moon. Cass shivers in her nightdress, trying to hang on to the thought of the Wadebridge family asleep next door, because she feels so totally alone in the darkness. At this silent hour it seems as if the darkness might speak, as if the rustling of trees might resolve itself into a voice, the cloud shapes become faces. If someone were down in the stableyard now, looking up, they would see her pale face at the window. She would be looking down like the girl in her dream, the nowhere girl.

In the yard early next morning, Cass sees that Pascal Duclos has arrived and is already at work, filling water-buckets. He is in his early twenties, tall like his grandfather, with quick, decisive movements. At first glance, Cass realizes that she has been expecting some grinning red-faced farm yokel, a French version of Eddie Grundy in *The Archers*, and reprimands

herself for thinking in stereotypes. Pascal isn't at all yokellish
She introduces herself to him. He has intelligent blue eyes in
strong-boned face, with dark brows, and brown hair cu
neatly. Cass has the impression of someone confident and
purposeful. She wonders again what Tante Eugénie ha
against him. It seems a bit extreme to carry on a wartim
argument through two generations.

Pascal is obviously well capable of taking charge of Mistral
Watching him lead the stallion out to the paddock, Cass i
ashamed by her own timidity. One curt reprimand and
quick slap with the stick make the stallion behave with respec
Cass has a painful bruise on her arm where Mistral nipped he
while she was taking off his bridle yesterday evening, but sh
can't imagine him daring to bite Pascal.

Pascal doesn't speak to her much beyond their quic
"hello", and she feels rather in awe of him. He works quickly
cleaning out two stables while Cass is still on her first, an
takes care of a feed delivery while Cass is filling hay nets. B
the time she's finished he has emptied all the paper sacks int
the storage bins.

"That's it for this morning, then." He smiles at her, sud
denly looking far less formidable. "I'll be back at five. Th
mare looks very near foaling, I think. If anything happer
you'd better phone me at home."

"Are you at home all day?" she asks, wondering what h
does.

"Yes," Pascal says, and as if this needs explaining he add
"I run my own business, as a printer. Or try to – it's not doin
too well at the moment. I can't afford the latest technolog
That's why I'm doing this extra work, to help pay the bill

You know what to look for, with the mare?"

"Not really." Cass feels appallingly ignorant, but Pascal explains in detail, writes down his phone number and goes out to his black Peugeot, passing Jilly and Keith Wadebridge as they come back from the *boulangerie*.

"Who's that?" Jilly asks Cass on the way upstairs. "Not your boyfriend over from England?"

"No!" Cass can't help laughing at the idea. "That's Pascal. He works with the horses."

"Oh, he's French? I should have guessed." Jilly becomes conspiratorial. "He's rather dishy, isn't he?"

"Do you think so?"

Cass wonders why everything Jilly says annoys her. In view of this she is surprised to find herself accepting a cup of coffee while Jilly gets a picnic together, and then making arrangements to accompany Jilly to Omaha Beach and the American war cemetery on Friday.

"I feel I ought to go, being so close," Jilly explains, "but it's not really the sort of place to take Sophie and Charles, is it? And Keith's not really that bothered."

"I might go there on my day off," Cass says, unguardedly. "I've never been before."

"Oh, if you're going, I'll come with you!" Jilly says. "It'd be better than going on your own, wouldn't it? And it would solve my transport problem."

Quite unaware of Cass's lack of enthusiasm, she is soon making plans about times and telling Keith what's been decided. Mentally kicking herself, Cass goes into her own flat to get some lunch.

7. Omaha

On Friday morning a postcard arrives for Cass, one of the *Fa[r]
Side* cartoons she likes.

*Dearest Casserole, I am downcasst! I was expecting casscades [of]
letters from you by now. You're only in France, not casstaway on [a]
desert island. I assume there's a post office somewhere near you. [I]
must casstigate you for your negligence.* Mon coeur est cassé
*(Yes, I've been using a dictionary!) Has there been some cassas[-]
trophe? Love and lots of kisses from Robbie. PS I hope you haven['t]
got some smoothie Gallic lover by now. Seriously! I really miss yo[u]
Please write today. X X X X X.*

Cass doesn't know whether to feel touched, exasperated o[r]
angry. Typical Robbie, trying this jokey style where a mor[e]
serious approach hasn't produced a response. Picturing hi[m]
working out his laborious puns, looking up words in a dic[-]
tionary, she feels mean. At the very least she should have sen[t]
him a postcard by now. But she feels annoyed with him fo[r]
sounding as if nothing has happened, not acknowledging tha[t]
she wants to split up; not even mentioning the accident vic[-]
tim, the young father in intensive care. What's happened t[o]
him? Is he alive, dead, or somewhere in between? Isn't tha[t]
important to Robbie?

She sighs and props the postcard on the dressing table wit[h]
the other one. Today, her free day, she had better send him [a]
card, though she doesn't know what to write. Something brie[f]

and impersonal will have to do. But, getting ready to go out, she can't help thinking fondly of Robbie, wishing he were here to go with her. His company is easy, relaxing, undemanding. He would find his way by instinct to the friendliest bar, the most sheltered spot on the beach, the best viewpoint; he would hold her hand, hug and kiss her, in his bear-like way. After so many evenings on her own, Cass feels in need of warmth and affection. Jilly's company is a poor substitute.

They leave together for Omaha Beach after two false starts and a protracted farewell to the children, as if Jilly is abandoning them for a month rather than a few hours. Keith is going to take them to the market at Villeneuve and then swimming in the afternoon. After stopping at the supermarket for picnic provisions, Jilly and Cass are on their way at last, Jilly navigating.

"Left here – no, I don't mean here, I mean the next one. Follow the sign for Arromanches – is that how you pronounce it? My French is awful – Should be any minute now. Here it is – yes, left. Oops! Nearly missed it. Now keep going –"

Cass resigns herself to a day of ceaseless chatter, blaming her own feebleness for getting into such a situation and for not finding an excuse to back out.

"Do you think that foal will be born today?" Jilly asks once they are safely heading for Arromanches. She keeps a forefinger carefully planted on the road atlas. "I do hope so. Sophie and Charles will be so thrilled. I hope it's born before we go home."

"It ought to be. Pascal thinks the next couple of days, or nights."

"How does he know so much about horses?"

"He used to work on a farm that bred Percherons, when he first left school," Cass says, having found out that much while she and Pascal mended a gap in one of the fences yesterday.

"So, do the two of you go off for long rides in the countryside?" Jilly asks, with a suggestive lift of one eyebrow.

Cass laughs. "No! They're all breeding horses, not used for riding. And I can't ride anyway. I expect Pascal can."

"He'd look good in riding clothes, wouldn't he?"

Cass can't imagine why Jilly is so interested, although she soon realizes that Jilly wants to question her about everyone. "So your aunt and uncle are pretty wealthy, then? What got your uncle started on the horses? I bet that house is lovely inside. Must be worth a fortune. So they haven't got any children of their own? Is that why they want you here?"

Cass is relieved to pull up at the Omaha Beach car park. There are a number of vehicles parked here already, with British and French numberplates, one Audi with a D plate: D for Deutschland. How does it feel to be a German visiting France, Cass wonders, especially here at the D-Day beaches with their strong associations of heroism and sacrifice, the overthrow of tyranny? The passing of the recent fifty-year anniversaries has brought the war closer, not farther away – there are new memorials, museums and marker posts marked *Voie de la Liberté 1944* all the way along this stretch of coast, which seems partly to belong to the British and the Americans who fought and died to regain it from the occupying Germans. Poppy wreaths adorn the memorials, placed there by blazered war veterans who come in coachloads to honour their dead companions. Cass has visited the British landing beaches farther along towards Ouistreham – Gold, Juno and

Sword – but this is the first time she has come to the famous American war cemetery.

Even Jilly is silenced by the vastness of the place, its quiet solemnity. There is a huge colonnaded monument, with American flags flying, and a formal rectangular pool below. Beyond, there are white crosses against greensward, rows and rows of them, each throwing its own shadow on the grass. Precisely placed and spotlessly white, as if each life had existed for no other reason than to fill its place in this vast pattern, the crosses lead the eye across a smooth brow of green, sloping away towards the beach. Cass leaves Jilly, drawn away from the monument along the main path, towards a circular stone chapel. She thinks this is the end of the cemetery, but as she reaches it she can see that there are as many graves again, reaching down to a belt of pines. Occasionally a Star of David marks the grave of a Jewish soldier, but otherwise the crosses are blank, anonymous. As Cass moves slowly down the rows, her perspective shifts so that the headstones flicker white on green, white on white, white on green, changing their patterns, forming grids, diagonals, stretching and diminishing far into the distance. It's difficult to understand the scale of so many graves, so many dead Americans.

She stops in front of one of the crosses beside the main path and closes her eyes. A smiling American soldier appears in front of her: blond, six-foot, with a wide grin that conceals an anxiety not to let himself down in front of his peers. His height and his broad shoulders conceal his immaturity; he has to live up to his physique. He has travelled halfway round the world to die here. Cass opens her eyes to look at the blank cross and wonders whether just one missing grave would spoil the pattern. If he had survived he would be in his early seventies now, an elderly man tending his garden in the United States, perhaps, sitting out on his verandah, reliving his memories. There would have been sons, daughters, grandchildren, people who have never had the chance to exist because Private Todd Lindley – the name flips up in her mind – was killed here by German fire in 1944, aged nineteen or so.

The breeze soughs through the belt of pines with a rushing sound, making her shiver. Jilly has stayed behind near the entrance, taking photographs, but now she hurries along to join Cass. "Incredible, isn't it?" she says breathlessly. "So many of them. Such an awful waste. Makes you think, doesn't it?"

"Yes."

Cass wishes Jilly had left her alone for a bit longer. Jilly's excited voice, the trite phrases, make it impossible to think. They walk slowly around the cemetery and look at the arrowed maps on the monument, and the garden of shrubs and trees. Jilly takes more photographs and then they go down over the low rugged cliff, through dunes to the beach. The tide is out, leaving a stretch of smooth, pale sand. An elderly couple are walking along hand-in-hand, and a boy throws a stick for a dog to retrieve. The coast curves round towards the Cotentin peninsula and Utah Beach. The scene is so tranquil that it's impossible to imagine the beach raked with shell-fire, troops swarming ashore, the sea dark with landing-craft, artillery fire crashing from the pill-boxes. Soldiers dying in the waves and on the sand. Here, on Omaha Beach, where Cass is standing, hundreds lay dying from their wounds. She tries to see it, really happening, but her imagination supplies only black-and-white newsreel.

Would Private Todd Lindley have thought it worth dying so that she can come here as a gawping sightseer? Words can't frame an adequate response; the scale of it makes her as inarticulate as Jilly. *So many of them. Such an awful waste. Makes you think, doesn't it?*

Pascal has already finished for the evening and left by the time Cass and Jilly arrive back. Jilly goes in to cook for her family; Cass, not hungry, collects an apple, puts on a jacket and goes out to the yard to look at the mare, who is in the foaling box, calmly eating hay. Cass is a little disappointed not to see Pascal. Presumably he doesn't expect the mare to foal tonight or he wouldn't have left so early. Although she wouldn't have wished for Maurice's accident to happen, she has to admit that Pascal's arrival has made life more interesting, now that she has got over her initial awe. At his instigation they have passed from the formality of *vous* to the friendlier *tu*, and now she likes him: his quick efficiency, his voice, his quiet confidence that strikes her as more truly masculine than the loud posturings of Robbie and Kelvin. And she wants him to like her.

It is starting to rain, a warm spring rain that dampens the dust in the yard and makes the grass and foliage smell greenly. Across the two nearer paddocks, she can see the yearlings grazing by the reserve hedge. She leans on the fence, enjoying the coolness of the rain and the warm dusk, watching them move about slowly as they browse. She is still thinking about D-Day, about the advances afterwards, reclaiming every wood and field and village from the army of occupation. Were the Germans here too, in St Privat, or was it such a rural backwater that they left it to its own devices? What was it like here in the war? What difference did it make to everyday life in St Privat when it was liberated? She thinks again of the quarrel between Gaston Duclos and her great-aunt. Seen against the enormous sacrifices of the D-Day landings, the campaign to win France back for the French, anything they could have argued over seems trivial, pointless. Weren't there more important things to worry about than petty jealousy? Couldn't they have got over it by now?

She gazes across the fields in the direction of the nature reserve, the cottage. Curiosity stirs inside her, but she isn't going there now, not in the twilight. She can resist that.

The sound of a car engine surprises her and she turns to see Pascal's black Peugeot drawing up in the yard. Cass is aware of a sharpening sense of pleasure as he gets out, carrying a big bag.

"Cass?" he calls. "What are you doing, standing there in the rain?"

Cass pushes back her hair and feels it webbed with dampness. "Nothing much. Just thinking. I thought you'd gone home."

"I did, to collect some things. I'm staying here tonight. For the mare."

"Oh! I thought – Where are you staying?"

He smiles and indicates the bag. "Camping in the harness-room. I've brought everything I need."

"Is she definitely going to have the foal, then?"

"Yes, I think so." Pascal stows his bag in the harness-room

and they stand together outside the mare's stable. "See the way she's lifting her tail, and the way the foal's moved in position slightly, her different shape, there? I think soon."

"Are you going to stay awake all night?"

"I've brought my sleeping bag, and an alarm clock. I'll set it and check her every hour."

"I could have kept an eye on her this evening, and phoned you if anything happened." Cass looks round at the sparse room, with its wooden cupboards, boxes of grooming kit, medicine box, trunks containing horse rugs. "You won't be very comfortable in here." She pauses. "I've got a sofa upstairs in my flat. Not very big, but you could sleep on that if you like. You can still come down and check when you need to. I could do alternate hours with you."

She is embarrassed by Pascal's hesitation, as if she's suggested something improper.

"Thank you," he says. "But it's probably best if I stay down here. I can keep the hatch open and I'll hear if anything starts to happen."

"I'd like to help, though. Would you call me, if she is going to have it?"

Pascal agrees, and starts getting things ready for the foaling: bales of straw, disinfectant, buckets, a kettle for hot water, a mash for the mare to have afterwards.

"Might something go wrong?" Cass asks. "Is that why you have to be here?"

"Usually it doesn't," Pascal says, spreading out rugs for a mattress under his sleeping bag, "but there can be problems. Mainly, if the foal's legs aren't in the right position, or its head is bent back."

"What would you have to do?"

"I'm not enough of an expert to do anything myself. Call a vet, probably. At least," Pascal says, "this mare has had foals before. She knows all about it."

Cass looks through the hatch. The mare is still quietly eating her hay, showing no signs of agitation.

"What are you going to do now?" She looks at her watch. "It's too early to go to sleep. Do you want to come up and have a drink?"

"That would be very nice, thank you."

Upstairs, Cass draws the curtains and turns on the lights. She makes filter coffee and opens a packet of biscuits, which is all she can find to offer him.

"You're the first guest I've had in here," she remarks.

"I'm privileged."

Dressed in jeans and a grey polo-neck jumper, Pascal looks incongruous sitting on the small flowered sofa, and she realizes that he is too tall to sleep on it in any comfort.

"Your uncle told me you've dropped out of school in England, is that right?" he asks her.

"Yes." She tells him about her illness and her reluctance to go back to school, but doesn't mention Robbie or the accident. Really, she is more interested in finding out about Pascal. She asks him about his printing business and he talks a little about the problems he is having, keeping costs down to compete with bigger firms.

"But I'm reluctant to give it up. It's a kind of family tradition," he says. "My grandfather used to run an underground printing press, here in the village."

"Your grandfather? You mean, in the war?"

"Yes. He used to print a newsletter, early on, when the Resistance was getting organized in the area."

Cass hesitates. Perhaps Pascal is the person who can answer her questions. But she doesn't know how to begin.

"Were there Germans here, in St Privat?" she asks.

"Yes." Pascal sips his coffee, looking at her. "Not just in the village. Here, in the house."

"*Really?* In my great-grandfather's house?"

Pascal nods. "They used to take over big houses, hotels, whatever they wanted, for billets. I don't suppose your great-grandfather wanted them but he wouldn't have had any choice. No one did."

Cass thinks of German soldiers sitting down to eat in the dining-room where she herself has eaten meals. German voices, talking, laughing, giving orders. What was it like to have your house taken over by German soldiers? Did the family share with the Germans, eat with them? Or were they treated as servants? There are dozens of questions she wants to ask. And Tante Eugénie was here then. Was that why Pascal's great-grandfather quarrelled with her, because there were Germans in the house? But that wasn't Eugénie's fault.

"Was that something to do with –" She hesitates to ask so directly, but asks anyway. "Something to do with my great-grandfather shooting himself? But no, it couldn't have been. That was after the Germans left, after the Liberation." An awful thought strikes her. "He wasn't a collaborator, was he? Was that why he killed himself after the Germans left?"

"No. Your great-grandfather wasn't a collaborator." He fidgets in his seat and looks at his watch. "I'd better go down and look at the mare."

"But it's not on the hour yet," Cass protests, wanting to know more.

"All the same. I'll just have a quick look."

He finishes his coffee and hurries downstairs. The flat seems very empty when he has gone. Cass washes the mugs, knowing that he has left to avoid answering any more of her questions.

8. Mistral

Cass wakes to her alarm at the usual time, realizing that she's slept through any night-time developments in the foaling box beneath. She pulls on her jeans and jumper quickly and hurries down. It is wet and windy, the rain coming in gusts. The mare is looking over her stable door, and there is no sign of Pascal.

In the harness-room she finds a note from him:

Cass – 5 a.m. and nothing happening. I've gone home for some sleep. See you later. Ring me if there are any problems meanwhile. Pascal.

His handwriting is small, firm and precise. She folds the note and puts it in her pocket to keep. She has let him down by not sharing the overnight vigil, but she can make up for it now by finishing all the morning chores before he comes back. She runs upstairs for her waterproof jacket and starts work, determined to be as quick and efficient as Pascal. She waters and feeds the horses, leads the mares out to the paddocks, decides to leave the pregnant mare where she is and gives her some hay.

The stallion is waiting to be taken out, but Cass welcomes the chance to show Pascal that she can cope. She has seen how he does it. Armed with the bridle and stick, she goes to Mistral's stable, where he has churned his bedding into a heap. He spins round excitedly as Cass goes in, knocking into her and making her lose her balance.

"No – no, you don't!" she tells him sharply. She is trying to convey authority, but she can't convince herself, let alone the horse. Mistral jerks his head high, out of her reach, and it takes several attempt to get the bridle on. She fastens the buckles with fumbling fingers. Now they're ready. The door swings open and the stallion launches himself out into the rain. A gust spatters in Cass's face and Mistral prances, excited by the weather.

"Walk – walk properly!" she instructs him.

He throws his head sideways, trying to jerk the lead rein from her grasp. He is only *méchant*, she remembers, not vicious. But out here in the wind, with the rain beating into her face and her vision misting, it's hard to believe that the stallion isn't driven by malevolence. He knows her weaknesses. Controlling him isn't as easy as Pascal makes it seem.

She takes a firmer grip. "Behave yourself!"

As they cross the yard in spurts and dashes, she realizes that she has forgotten to open the gate first. The bolt is stiff and she needs both hands to dislodge it. While she struggles, the stallion barges into her from behind, crushing her against the metal gate. His teeth close on her forearm in a sharp nip.

"Oh, you –!"

Angered by the pain, she turns on him. Mistral rears, playfully, but enough to frighten her, his front hooves dangerously close to her face. She gives a desperate tug and the bolt slides back. Almost falling through, she lurches into the churned mud of the gateway and the stallion plunges after her. She can't get her feet out of the mud quickly enough to avoid him. He turns on her, rearing, huge, filling the sky in front of her. A forefoot strikes out and she feels the glancing pain as it brushes the side of her face. She staggers back against the gate and the lead rein slips from her grasp.

"Cass! Cass!"

A blurred figure is running at the edge of her vision. Pascal. She sees his car pulled up at the yard gate, the driver's door open. As he reaches her the stallion dives away, galloping round his paddock in a triumphant display of bucks and leaps, his lead rein flying. Shakily, Cass leans against the gate, her eyes stinging with tears of shock and frustration. She has let herself down. In front of Pascal, who she wants so badly to impress.

Pascal sloshes through the muddy gateway. "What are you doing, stupid girl? Why didn't you wait for me?"

His reprimand is more than she can take. Biting her lip, she turns away. She feels as if she's escaped from a mugging and all he can do is tell her off. She wipes her eyes angrily, determined not to cry.

"Are you all right?" Pascal says more gently. "Here, show me your face –"

Grudging, she turns towards him. He puts one hand on her shoulder and smooths the fingers of the other over her cheekbone. His face is very close to hers, concerned. She notices his dark lashes, his blue eyes with darker grey rims to the pupils, his lips slightly parted as he examines her cheek.

"He struck out at you?"

"Yes. I couldn't get out of the way."

"You're going to have quite a bruise there. Does it hurt?"

"More numb than hurting. He bit me as well." She rubs her forearm. "And knocked me against the gate."

"I'm sorry. Sorry. I didn't mean to shout at you," Pascal

says. "You've had a shock. Come inside and sit down." He glances at the stallion, who is still rampaging around, neighing shrilly. "He can wait. I'll try to catch him later." He takes her arm and guides her through the gateway, yanking it closed behind them.

"I only wanted to save you the bother," Cass says, as they walk slowly towards the harness-room. "I wasn't sure how long you'd be. And what about your day off? I'll need to manage by myself then."

"It wasn't your fault. That stallion doesn't get enough handling. He's getting above himself." Pascal looks at her. "Don't do it again, will you promise me? Not unless I'm here."

Cass nods. She doesn't intend to try again, although the question of Pascal's day off is unanswered. In the harness-room, he sits her down on the pile of horse rugs, where his sleeping bag is still spread out. "Now show me that bite."

She takes off her waterproof and rolls up her right sleeve. Pascal sits beside her and takes her hand, holding out her arm to look at the purpling red marks. His grip on her hand is warm and firm. The indentations of the stallion's teeth are clearly visible but the skin is unbroken. Pascal touches the blemish with careful, sensitive fingertips. He breathes in sharply.

"He needs a good lesson, that one. More bruises, but no actual wound. It's lucky you had your waterproof on. How are you feeling?" He rolls down her sleeve and releases her hand. "Still shaken up?"

"I'm fine. Thank you. I'll start on the stables now," Cass says.

"No, you won't." Pascal gets up to rummage in the medicine cupboard. "First you're going upstairs to bathe those bruises. There's some liniment in here somewhere – I saw it yesterday. And then I'm going to make you some coffee and you're going to sit down for a few minutes and recover properly. The stables can wait."

Later, when Cass is sweeping the yard, she sees Pascal in the stallion's paddock. He has caught Mistral and is giving him a leading lesson, making him walk, stand, wait, walk forward steadily. The rain is still lashing down but Pascal is intent on his task.

When he's gone, Cass goes up to her flat to make lunch for herself. There is hardly anything to eat in the kitchen, and she makes do with an apple, a piece of cheese and a stale *brioche*, thinking over the events of the morning. Now that she doesn't have to keep up a pretence for Pascal, she feels shaken from her battering by the stallion. And shaken in a quite different way by Pascal's concern for her afterwards. She can still feel the gentle touch of his fingers on her cheek, on her arm, like a caress.

She goes to the bathroom mirror and looks at her bruised face. The mark on her cheekbone is deep-down, a faint reddish-purple bruising which will doubtless emerge and turn multicoloured later. She lifts her hand to touch where Pascal touched, and the skin tingles as it did then. What would have happened if she had allowed herself to cry? Would he have taken her in his arms, held her close? And then she mocks herself for being so stupid, fantasizing like this, just because he was kind to her, as anyone else would have been. Pascal is

quite right; she is stupid, though not in the way he meant a
the time. He is six or seven years older than her and he
probably thinks of her as a silly schoolgirl, a child who ha
fallen down and hurt herself, no more. She lets her hair loose
from its ponytail and brushes it so that it falls softly on each
side of her face. It is Cécile looking back at her from the
mirror, a young woman, not a child. Usually she sees only the
faults in her appearance – her nose isn't quite straight, her
eyebrows are too heavy. But now, in the dim light of the
bathroom, pretending to look at a stranger, she can see that
Cécile's face has all the ingredients of attractiveness. She
hopes it's Cécile that Pascal sees, the bruise heightening the
mystery of her shadowy eyes, not Cass with her clothes that
smell of horse. . .

To make herself stop thinking about him, she finds the
postcard she bought yesterday for Robbie and still hasn't
written. It shows the American memorial at Omaha Beach
hardly a match for the jokey cartoon he sent her. *Dear Robbie*
she writes, and then sits fiddling with a strand of hair and
gazing out of the window for several minutes. She can't help
looking at her watch to check that it's only seven hours until
Pascal comes back to do his evening jobs. And then he wil
have to stay all night again for the mare – but the postcard i
still blank. She writes: *I am enjoying my work here. I visited*
Omaha Beach on my day off yesterday. My flat above the stables i
lovely and I work with someone called Pascal who – She wishe
she hadn't started on that bit. She considers various alter
natives and writes, lamely, *is very nice. There's a bird reser*
next to the stud where I go for walks sometimes. Thanks for you
cards, Cass.

It is hopelessly bland, the sort of thing she might write out of duty to a distant relative. But Robbie seems distant now, part of a different life. What else can she do? She can't tell him the truth. She has told him the truth already and he won't believe it.

At two o'clock she drives to the *Intermarché* supermarket in the village. She buys eggs, cheeses, *charcuterie* meats, fruit, and then adds mineral water and a bottle of wine. Returning her trolley to the collection point she sees Gaston Duclos, Pascal's grandfather, with a carrier bag of shopping and his raincoat collar turned up against the drizzle. He raises his hand in salute, and she waves back, pleased that he has acknowledged her. He could have pretended not to see her, turned away, as he did on the church porch. Cass remembers Pascal's remark about what he did in the war, working for the Resistance as a printer. Did Pascal mean that the printing press was *literally* underground, in a cellar, hidden from the Germans who drove into the village from Le Clos d'If? Perhaps Tante Eugénie had accidentally revealed its whereabouts to the Germans, and that was why Gaston Duclos had quarrelled with her. But, if it had been discovered, surely he would have been deported or executed? Pascal sounded proud when he spoke of the family tradition, suggesting that the printing had continued undetected. Cass imagines the dangerous excitement of defying the Germans, organizing a Resistance group under their noses. Whispered conversations in the café, messages slipped from hand to hand, secret meetings. Familiar enough through the glamorizing eye of the film camera; terrifying, she imagines, in real life. Would she have been brave enough, she wonders, if she had lived here then? Or would she have had a weak spot, a pressure point, that would make her reveal a crucial secret, betray someone, label herself a collaborator?

She gets into her car and starts the ignition, thankful that it's a test she will never have to face.

9. Speaking in English

It has been agreed that Cass will keep an eye on the pregnant mare during the evening and that Pascal won't come back until ten o'clock unless Cass detects some change. When he arrives, he checks the mare, gets everything ready in the harness-room and comes up to Cass's flat for coffee, and they end up sharing a bottle of wine and talking, well after midnight.

"I ought to take advantage of you being here," Pascal says, "by practising my English. I can speak enough to be understood but I don't practise enough. Let's speak English tonight. You must correct me when I make mistakes."

He is sitting on the sofa, Cass on the floor, not too close. "All right," she says, pleased because it gives her the opportunity to question him with a directness she wouldn't contemplate in French. She moves round to face him, as if it's an interrogation. "Are you hungry?"

"No, I have eaten at home."

"How old are you?"

"I have twenty-four years."

"I *am* twenty-four, you should say. Where do you live?"

"I live in Villeneuve, six kilometres from here in the direction Villers-Bocage. You should come to visit one time."

"Thank you, I'd like to." Cass stores this away with private pleasure, wondering how much to read into it. "What's your house like?"

"It is quite old. Not much big, but enough big for us."

"Not *very* big, but big enough for us," Cass correct automatically, her thoughts locking on to the *us*. Us? "Yo don't live by yourself?"

"No, I live with my wife and young baby."

Cass is sure that her dismay must be blindingly obvious. ' didn't realize you were married," she says. The words com out flat with disappointment, in spite of her effort to soun light and conversational.

"Yes, I am married two years."

"I've *been* married two years. What is your wife's name?"

"Monique. And our son is called Gilles. He is one year.'

Cass turns away to sip at her wine, her feelings in turmoi She tries to assimilate the knowledge that Pascal is a husban and father, not single as she has foolishly supposed. Wh hasn't the possibility occured to her? She hasn't even won dered whether he has a girlfriend, let alone a wife; since th morning, she has been daft enough to imagine that he's bee waiting for her to turn up in his life. She's been such an idio He isn't available: he is Monique's husband. Lucky Monique

Utterly deflated, she doesn't trust herself to ask any mor questions about his private life. "Your English isn't bad," sh says, although they've hardly discussed anything ver demanding so far.

"But I don't have the vocabulary. That's why I am needin to practise."

Cass wonders why it is that English spoken by a French man, however badly, sounds charming, whereas Englis people speaking bad French only sound incompetent. Sh decides to change the subject before she gives herself awa entirely, embarrassing both of them.

"That's why I need to practise," she corrects. "Do you ever go into the bird reserve?"

"Sometimes I have been there. I am not – *bien informé?* – about birds. Do you go there?"

"Knowledgeable. Yes, sometimes. But I haven't got any binoculars."

"Binoculars?" Pascal queries.

"*Jumelles.* For birdwatching."

"Oh, yes. I can borrow them for you."

"Thank you – I'd like that." Cass watches his hand cradling the glass and tries not to think of him with Monique, eating a meal with her, kissing her goodbye. She sees Monique as small and dark, standing at the front door holding up the baby boy to wave as Pascal drives away. Does Monique mind him spending two nights in succession away from home? Sitting here drinking wine in someone else's flat? But Cass doesn't want to think about Monique. Deliberately, she turns her thoughts to the mysteries she is trying to unravel. "Pascal, you know the quarrel my great-aunt had with your grandfather during the war? Do you know what it was about?"

He hesitates for slightly too long before answering, "No."

"You do!"

"Yes then, I do. But it was since very long ago. It should be forgotten now."

"Oh, please tell me, Pascal! I need to know!" She sits forward, embracing her knees. "There are so many secrets here! And everyone knows except me. It was something to do with the Germans in the house, wasn't it?"

"Yes, it was."

"Someone was a collaborator? But not my great-grandfather. Why did he kill himself? Do you know that, too? Does everyone know?"

"No. Not everyone. But my family is more –" Pascal struggles for the word he needs. "I don't have the English words. It's too – too *compliqué*."

"In French then. Your family was more involved?" Cass prompts, switching. "Because your grandfather was going to marry Tante Eugénie? What happened to make them break it off?"

Pascal's expression becomes obstinate. "I can't tell you. It's not fair. It's better forgotten."

Cass wonders what he would say if she told him about her dreams, her intuitions. "But I'm involved, too!"

"That's what I mean. It's your family and mine."

His glance holds hers for a moment. Cass looks away with difficulty. "If they'd got married, we'd be related, wouldn't we? Second cousins, or something?"

Pascal nods. "But then we wouldn't be the same people."

Cass remembers the theory she dismissed earlier. "Was it my aunt who collaborated? Did she tell the Germans about your grandfather being in the Resistance?"

"No. He was never captured."

"Please! It's like banging my head against a wall! What did she do, then?"

"Oh –" Pascal flops against the back of the sofa as if in surrender. "I expect you can work it out for yourself. She was – nineteen, twenty, a beautiful girl, according to my grandfather – with young German officers billeted in the house . . ."

Cass stares at him. "You mean she . . ." She doesn't know how to put it. "You mean she – they – Do you mean they mistreated her, raped her or something? But then no one would blame her for that, would they? Or do you mean she –" Her thoughts plunge off in a different direction. "Is it something to do with the cottage in the reserve? Did she go there to meet a German boyfriend, something like that?"

Pascal's eyes meet hers, flaring in surprise.

"The cottage? No, I don't think so."

"What, then? *Something* happened at that cottage, didn't it? I know it did!"

"How do you know about the cottage?"

Cass turns her wineglass in her fingers, looking down at it. "I don't know how I know. But I do."

And he knows something, too; he has as much as admitted it. He is looking troubled by the turn the conversation has taken. Any minute now he will bolt off downstairs to look at the mare, she can tell; she is driving him away again.

"Where did my great-grandfather shoot himself?" she asks.

"Not at the cottage, if that's what you think. In the house. Cass, you are asking a great deal too many questions," he says gently. "Let's go back to English. It's safer."

In the early hours of the morning Cass wakes to the realization that something is happening in the foaling box underneath her bedroom. Looking out of the window she sees light shining on the concrete from the harness-room window and the stable. Maybe Pascal is only doing his hourly check, but glancing at her watch she sees that it is half-past two. Only an hour and a half since Pascal left her for his spartan sleeping-quarters below. Having had to adjust her ideas about him so comprehensively, she felt too embarrassed to repeat her offer of the sofa, although she's sure it must be cold and damp in the harness-room.

She dresses quickly and goes down. Pascal is in the foaling box, standing just inside the door. A newly-born foal is lying on the straw, its coat dark and wet, and the mare is standing over it, licking it.

"Oh, Pascal! I wanted to be here!"

"It's only just born, twenty minutes ago. It all happened so quickly that I didn't have time to come up and call you."

"Did you have to do anything?"

"Not really. It was very easy. They're both fine."

Cass's disappointment is hollow in her stomach. If it were so easy, then he could have spared two minutes to come upstairs and tell her. She wonders whether the real reason is that he didn't want to come up to her bedroom. She has been so transparent that Pascal would have to be particularly dimwitted not to realize how interested she is in him. Still is, in spite of his being married; she can't help it. And he isn't in the least dimwitted.

"Will it be able to stand up by itself? What do we have to do now?"

"It will stand in a little while," Pascal says. "We don't need to interfere yet. But we need to be sure that the foal knows how to suckle. Sometimes they don't."

The foal jerks its neck and raises a whiskery muzzle. The mare's licking slowly dries its coat from a dark liver-colour to soft brown; its head is small and shapely, the forehead babyishly domed. When the foal is thoroughly dry, the mare nudges it gently with her nose. It props its forelegs in front, heaves itself up, sways on bent legs and then totters, collaps sing in the straw. A second attempt results in a nose-dive. Each time the mare whickers softly and nudges it, encouraging it to try again. She knows it must learn to stand.

At last the foal is up, unsure on wobbly legs. The mare nudges it round to her udder and soon, more confident on its feet, the foal starts to blunder around her, seeking. Pascal moves closer to guide it and before long the foal is suckling. Its knee and hock joints are huge, in long legs ridiculously out of proportion to the tiny frame of its body and its short neck. Its tuft of a tail waggles as it begins to drink with enthusiasm.

"A filly," Pascal says. "Your uncle will be pleased. His stallion's first foal."

"Mistral's daughter," Cass says. She is amazed by the strength of the foal's instincts – an hour old, standing, and feeding herself. In the wild she would be able to gallop with the herd at a few hours old. It's a small miracle – commonplace enough, but a miracle all the same.

Pascal boils a kettle for the mare's mash and brings her a full hay net, and Cass forks the soiled straw into a barrow and wheels it away. There is a special heater-lamp in the foaling box which Pascal says must be left on to provide extra warmth against the chilly April night.

"You can turn it off first thing in the morning, unless it's very cold." He looks suddenly tired, yawning, and Cass realizes that he probably hasn't slept at all. "They'll be all right now. I'm going home to sleep. Thanks, Cass, for your help." He touches her arm briefly. She senses his pride in having officiated successfully at the birth of this perfect creature, and she is warmed with satisfaction at having shared at least some of it with him, although she has done very little. "I'll be back at the usual time," he says, "so don't try to put the stallion out. You can tell your uncle about the foal – a nice surprise for him."

He leaves, and Cass goes back to bed for a few hours' sleep. She has seen the strength of instinct in the mare and foal and now her own instincts are aroused: her desire to be held and loved, to love in return. Her bed is too big, too empty. She lies awake thinking of Pascal arriving home, getting into bed with Monique, receiving her sleepy embrace. He will tell her about the foal, his arms around her in the dawn light, his mouth against her hair. Lucky Monique.

The Wadebridge children are excited by the foal, clustering round the stable. Jilly holds Sophie up to see over the half-door.

"We must be very quiet," Pascal warns them. "The foal is only born since a few hours. We must make no noise to fright them."

"How big will she be when she grows up?" Charles whispers.

"Like her mother," Pascal says. "Not very much big. The stallion is taller than the mother but not so big for a pure-blood."

"Thoroughbred," Cass says, trying not to smile at his misphrasings. She loves the way he speaks English.

Cass cleans out the stable as best she can around the mare and foal. They will stay inside until the foal is stronger, and then they will be turned out for a few hours each day, if it's warm enough, in a paddock by themselves. Oncle Gérard comes down, dressed in his suit for church, to see the foal.

Tante Eugénie hasn't asked Cass to go to church this time, although she is expected for lunch later. The foal is to be named *Mousson*, Monsoon, after her sire, and Cass wonders whether Oncle Gérard is planning a whole string of windy names for the stallion's next crop.

"Keep an eye on that black mare," she hears him telling Pascal, "in case she comes into season again. She may not have held."

"What does he mean?" Cass asks Pascal when her uncle has gone off to church.

"He means she may not be pregnant," Pascal answers shortly. He is busy with the stallion, about to give him another leading lesson. "Don't worry about my day off tomorrow," he adds, looking at her. "I can easily come over to take Mistral out and bring him in again. I don't want you to do it yourself until he's learned better manners."

His wording puts the blame firmly on the stallion, not on Cass. She tries not to be too obviously pleased that she will see Pascal on his day off, even if only for a few minutes. She trusts him not to bully the stallion too firmly into submission. In spite of her fear and her bruises, she knows that the stallion's arrogant maleness is part of his beauty.

The bruise on her face has come up gloriously purple, making her look as if she's been in a street brawl. Tante Eugénie comments on it when Cass goes up to the house for lunch.

"That stallion!" She glances at her husband. "He is a menace!"

"He means no harm. It's a pity about Cass's face but that bruise will soon go," Oncle Gérard says evenly. "And it proves I was right to hire young Pascal. How are you getting on with him?" he asks Cass.

"Oh, fine," she says, hoping she isn't blushing.

"He's a good chap with the horses, I'll say that for him. He'll soon have that stallion knowing who's in charge. And he's put in a lot of hours over the foaling."

"Yes. When will Maurice be coming back?" Cass asks, shamelessly hoping it won't be for a while yet.

Oncle Gérard shakes his head doubtfully. "I don't know. At his age, it's not funny to break bones."

"Those horses!" Tante Eugénie says again. "I don't know why you don't sell them and take up golf. It would be a lot less expensive, as well as less dangerous."

"But not as rewarding. And now that we've got the first foal from my new stallion – who knows? This could be the start of a famous bloodline."

The new foal's health is toasted in Muscadet and even Tante Eugénie says she might come down to the stables later to have a look. During the meal, Cass looks at her aunt with a new interest, picturing the beautiful girl of fifty years ago. The bone structure is still there, the fine skin beneath layers of make-up. There is a self-awareness and pride in her bearing that must have been eye-catching in a girl. Cass wonders what Tante Eugénie could tell her if she chose to. This room can't have changed much since German soldiers were billeted in the house. They would have sat here, on the same chair, perhaps eating off the same china, while Tante Eugénie served at table. Did the Germans flatter her with their attentions? Was there a special one, young, handsomely Teutonic, catching her eye as she filled his wineglass? Cass pictures her aunt strolling in the garden with her German lover, learning each other's language. Perhaps it had been a way of drawing attention away from the Resistance workers in the village: pretending she had nothing to do with them, keeping a foot in each camp. But Gaston Duclos has never forgiven her for whatever she did. Cass has seen pictures of young French women who had German boyfriends: paraded in the street to be jeered at, their heads shaved. Is that what happened to Tante Eugénie, after the Liberation?

It's no use asking. Tante Eugénie has a way of shutting herself off, her eyes guarded behind their hooded lids. She is too careful to let herself slip, however roundabout the questioning. If the beautiful girl of fifty years ago is still there, she is kept well under control inside the stiff, smartly-dressed woman. Cass realizes that she hardly knows her aunt; since arriving here, she has spoken more to Oncle Gérard, in their daily conversations about the lawnmower, the mares, the feed supplies. Tante Eugénie is remote, concerned only with her garden and her spiritual life: her three times weekly attendance at Mass, her devotions. Her Madonna figurines, one outside the house and one in, as if Tante Eugénie wants an eye kept on her wherever she goes, to remind her to cross herself and murmur a prayer. What is she atoning for?

The lunchtime chatter, the Calvados and coffee, the mood of celebration, can't disguise the real atmosphere of the house. Cass feels as if she is sitting in a deep shadow cast by the war years. There are secrets everywhere, here particularly. They are in the air like motes of dust, glistening, teasing, ungraspable. Their presence is so strong that it feels as if the house is still occupied.

10. Dusk

"Here. These are for you." Pascal, about to leave, reaches into the passenger seat of his car and hands Cass a small pair of binoculars. "They're not mine, but you can borrow them while you're here."

"Oh – thanks!" Cass is touched by his thoughtfulness. The binoculars have only been mentioned once, but still he's remembered. It's his day off, and he has driven over to put the stallion out and look at the mare and foal. He didn't have to do either of those things, and Cass is grateful. Last night, missing him, she wished there were twenty more foals to be born. She knows she ought to give up her romantic thoughts about him, but they can still be friends, can't they? And Pascal's gesture seems to confirm it.

A letter from home arrives for Cass that day.

Thanks for your postcards, Mum writes. *I'm glad you like your flat and seem to be enjoying your work. I hope you're not tiring yourself too much, but I'm sure Tante Eugénie and Oncle Gérard will be careful not to overwork you, knowing you've been ill. Have you heard from Robbie? Dad met him in town yesterday, and there is good news about the man in hospital – he's out of intensive care now and in an ordinary ward, much to everyone's relief. I felt so sorry for his wife and children while it was all so uncertain. Robbie says that Kelvin's going to be prosecuted for reckless driving and will certainly be disqualified. I expect Robbie will write to you himself. He's having to work hard now for his A-levels...*

But the letter from Robbie doesn't arrive until Friday, and when it does Cass puts it in her bag without opening it, unsure whether she can face more of Robbie's reproaches. She will read it later. It's her day off, and she drives into Bayeux to see the tapestry and wander around the close, narrow streets and squares of the town, being a tourist for the day. The interior of the Cathedral is cool and shadowy, the flagstones of the floor seeming to exhale cold air. On an impulse, she finds coins for a candle and lights it, watching the small flame flicker blue then yellow, joining the others already burning. Something about the tranquillity of the Cathedral makes her uneasy. It is a sanctuary to some, no doubt, but she thinks of it standing here powerless throughout the war years, a serene island in an ocean of conflict, with German boots pounding the streets outside.

Usually she doesn't mind being on her own, but today she wishes she had someone to be with, to exclaim over the details of the tapestry, to have lunch with. There is plenty to see in Bayeux but by mid-afternoon, tired of sightseeing, she drifts into a café and sits down. The waiter taking her order looks startled and she realizes it's because of her face: the bruise on her cheekbone has worked its way through a whole spectrum of colours and has now reached jaundice yellow, tinged with purple. She wished she had remembered and sat in a shadowy corner.

A man and wife coming to sit at a nearby table with a bustle of coats and shopping look at Cass curiously, as if she has no right to be there, as if the world belongs to couples, families, people in groups. She feels intensely alone as it occurs to her that no one knows where she is at this moment, and probably no one cares much. She thinks: *I am like the nowhere girl. I have cut myself off from everyone, because I wanted to. And now I've succeeded. A bit too well.*

She reaches into her bag for a tissue and sees Robbie's letter, remembering her mother's news about the man in hospital. She is relieved to hear that he isn't going to die, but that doesn't actually – in a moral sense – make the incident any less serious; he *could* have died, could have been killed outright. Kelvin and the others didn't care enough. Or is she being unreasonable? Shouldn't she be pleased for Robbie, pleased that he wasn't seriously hurt in the accident and can put it down to experience? Perhaps she isn't being fair to Robbie at all. He has a way of making her feel mean, unappreciative. And perhaps he has a point.

She takes out the letter and opens it.

Thanks for the card, it says, rather huffily. *I hope it didn't take you too long to write it. I suppose you're too busy carting barrows of manure about to bother writing to me. You will be pleased to hear that David Thwaite – the guy in the Granada – is out of intensive care and likely to make a full recovery. So you can stop treating me as a murderer. I even thought of going in to visit him, but he might punch me on the nose if he's fit enough. Kelvin's facing charges, reckless driving, but he's relieved it's not going to be causing death by reckless driving. He's having a party on Saturday week – his eighteenth birthday – and if you were here you could have come. Course, it's not too far for you to pop back for the weekend if you really wanted to. You needn't even bring your car, to make it cheaper. Just get a passenger ticket and I'll pick you up at Portsmouth. Give me a ring if you fancy coming. Yours, still, though*

God knows why and don't bank on it for ever, because you don't deserve me, Robbie. PS Nothing to look forward to now but swotting for the exams, so you might spare me some sympathy. PPS Who's this Pascal guy?

"You must be joking!" Cass murmurs. Go all the way back to England, just to go to Kelvin's party! Kelvin is the last person she wants to see. They seem like little boys, Kelvin, Tim and Andy; Robbie too, when he's with them. She feels in need of company, but a sweaty, beery party with thumping music and couples groping in the bedrooms doesn't appeal to her in the least. Even though it was at just such a party that she started going out with Robbie.

It was an end-of-year barbecue at someone's house, after the GCSEs. It was supposed to be for year eleven only, but Robbie, who was already in the lower sixth, had wangled his way in with Kelvin. Cass knew Robbie by sight, knew that his name was Robbie McIntyre and that he was easy-going and a bit clownish and a lot of the girls liked him, but she had never spoken to him before.

It was his dancing that first attracted her. He was such a good mover that she couldn't stop watching him. He was supple and slack-jointed, reminding her of a stringed puppet. Not taking himself in the least seriously, he abandoned himself to the pleasure of the music and his own ingenuity. He caught Cass's eye a few times as he gyrated and eventually he danced over the grass towards her and pulled her with him, infecting her with his sense of rhythm. She couldn't match his style but it didn't matter; she laughed at him and enjoyed herself. When she told him her name, he repeated, "Cass? Short for casserole?"

And then she seemed to be going out with him. It was easy. Robbie didn't stammer or dither like some boys she had been out with; he didn't make a big thing about it, never became intense or demanding. He just kept turning up. He was fun to be with; attractive, too, with his corn-coloured hair kept deliberately tousled, his wide smile, his humorous brown eyes. There was something endearingly puppyish about him. For all his physical co-ordination when dancing, he was surprisingly clumsy in other ways – tripping over doormats, knocking glasses off tables, dropping keys from his pockets and losing them.

"It's like having a great lolloping sheepdog around the place," Cass teased him.

She had never much liked Kelvin. Kelvin was a sharp-faced, good-looking boy – *too* good-looking – with none of Robbie's likeable self-mockery. His sense of humour was sometimes just stupid, like Robbie's, but often barbed and cynical, sneering. Robbie would never accept any criticism of Kelvin. "He's my mate. He's all right," was his invariable defence. Kelvin was reputedly very brainy – unlike Robbie – but was too idle to bother much with his studies. He would get by, Cass supposed, because people like him usually did. He had a streetwise sharpness that made up for his casual approach to work.

Robbie was much nicer without Kelvin. When they were together, Robbie affected some of Kelvin's tough non-chalance. Robbie on his own was much more genuine: kind-hearted, always cheerful, reliable in his own way. Cass's mum loved him. He could always make her laugh, talking Inspector Clouseau French and bringing out a frivolous, girlish side of Mum that Cass rarely saw otherwise.

Robbie seemed more like Cass's brother than her boyfriend at times. Even when they kissed and hugged each other it was just fun: something nice to do, warm and reassuring. Remembering, Cass knows it's not enough now. She wants more than friendship and familiarity. Although she liked Robbie's straightforwardness at first, she realizes now that there's nothing much beneath the surface: nothing deep or secretive, nothing particularly thoughtful. His sunny personality appealed to Cass – the old Cass – but now Cécile sees only the bumbling puppy. For Robbie she is only Cass, Casserole. Her half-Frenchness (half-Frog, he calls her) gives rise to jokes about berets, strings of onions and snails in garlic. She is someone to joke with, listen to music with, be with, someone whose mum will always give him a meal whenever he turns up or let him crash out after a party. Cass wonders whether he recognizes the Cécile side of her at all.

Driving the last kilometre from the village, Cass passes Pascal in his car, going home. He waves but does not stop. Disappointment makes her sag, her hands heavy on the wheel; it's no use pretending that she wasn't hoping to see him.

Everything is quiet in the yard. Pascal has evidently decided that it's warm enough to leave the mares out for the night, apart from Mélodie and her foal; they are grazing contentedly by the far hedge. Cass goes up to her flat but feels too restless to stay indoors. The binoculars Pascal brought her are standing on the kitchen windowsill. Picking them up and turning them over in her hand, she decides to go out to the reserve. Not to the cottage – fear shivers down her spine as she remembers her panic. She isn't going there at this time of day, so close to dusk, but she will go birdwatching, and prove to herself that the pull of the cottage can be resisted.

Although she's hungry, she can't be bothered to cook herself a meal. She takes a piece of Camembert from the fridge and eats it as she walks slowly down the lane to the reserve entrance. There is one car parked there, a white Renault. Remembering her aunt's warnings, she wonder whether she has more to fear from solitary Renault-drivers in this remote place than from her own imaginings. She doesn't want to meet anyone on the reserve, but she isn't going to let herself be deterred by a harmless birdwatcher. Passing the car she notices a briefcase on the passenger seat and concludes that its owner has come straight from work. For some reason that makes her less wary and she enters the reserve, walking round the lake in a clockwise direction to break the pattern, so that it won't be like her dream.

It is a quiet, calm evening. After showers early in the day the air smells of damp soil and young foliage. Occasionally the loud *Pruk!* of a coot echoes across the lake and once Cass hears the ripple of a fish darting. The belt of scrubby woodland to her left is tinted with spring colours: hawthorn leaves almost fully out with flower buds in greenish clusters, the green-blue of poplars behind, a frosting of wild cherry. Where the trees are thicker and the ground is damp there are early bluebells, and Cass imagines she can smell their cool blueness on the air. Everything is growing, breathing. Being.

She can just see the battered roof of the cottage above its

trees, but she grips her binoculars as if they are her anchor to normality and turns her gaze firmly on the slatted hide ahead. She expects to see the other birdwatcher there, but the flaps are down. Inside, her footsteps sound hollow on the raised wooden floor. She opens the flaps and sits on the bench.

The hide is well positioned. There is an area of wild plants in front, an area of mud and shallows, and then the lake, widening and spreading into its various inlets. The cottage can't be seen from here. Cass has no bird book but there is a chart on the wall identifying various species of water bird. Adjusting her binoculars, she applies herself to the task of scanning the water and banks, identifying what she can see. Early swallows skimming the water. A pair of shelducks resting among the reeds; one grebe; an assortment of ducks. If Dad were here he'd see birds where she overlooks them – camouflaged against pebbles, scurrying through reeds – his telescope searching inexhaustibly.

When her eyes start to ache Cass lowers the binoculars and looks out at the scene before her. While she has sat here, daylight has changed to dusk. A faint mist is rising over the lake and the sky behind the poplars is a wash of deep pink, streaked with indigo cloud, the moon rising like a transparent silver coin. The air smells of water and mist and earth. The spring evening is a presence around her, touching and soothing all her senses. And deep inside her is an ache of longing that nothing can cure.

11. Breakout

Over the next few days, Cass is wary of Pascal. She doesn't ask him any further questions, or invite him up to her flat when they take a break from work. Her feelings shouldn't even be acknowledged, let alone encouraged. She gets on with her work and he gets on with his. With the mares now out to grass, the morning stable routine takes far less time. Cass is directed to jobs in the garden, and Pascal works with the stallion each morning for forty minutes or so, sometimes leading him out for road exercise, sometimes long-reining him in the paddock. He grooms the stallion every day and asks Cass to do it on his day off.

"Tie him up first to stop him nipping you. He won't give you any trouble now."

He also gets Cass to practise leading Mistral up and down the yard. With Pascal present, the stallion behaves himself, walking beside her with only the merest hint of a prance or sidestep.

"He's getting better," Pascal says. "Stallions ought to be handled properly, not treated as wild animals. We'll have to make him look smart tomorrow. Your uncle's got a visitor coming, some wealthy stud owner who's thinking of sending a couple of mares next season."

For the visit, Cass cleans the stallion's best in-hand bridle, polishing the bit, and Pascal grooms Mistral thoroughly, oiling his hooves and brushing out his mane and tail until they glisten, paler grey than his coat. Pascal tidies himself up too, to act as stud groom for the occasion. He puts on clean boots and combs his hair, squinting into a broken mirror in the harness-room.

Half an hour late, Oncle Gérard comes importantly into the yard with his guest, Monsieur Delacourt. The visitor is a portly man of fifty or so, smartly dressed in an expensive tweedy suit. Evidently used to treating stable hands as inferior beings, he doesn't address a single word to Pascal, even though it's Pascal who brings the stallion out to the yard and makes him stand and stretch out his neck as if he's being judged at a show.

"Have your man trot him up, could you?" Monsieur Delacourt says to Oncle Gérard, as if Pascal can't be spoken to.

Cass hates him for treating Pascal as if he's invisible. Pascal is just as well worth looking at as the horse, in her opinion. He trots Mistral up and down the yard and then stands in silence while Monsieur Delacourt walks slowly round, looking at the horse's short muscular back, his hocks, running a hand down his shoulder. Cass hopes Mistral will nip him, but of course Pascal wouldn't let him. *Your man!* Of all the cheek!

"That will do." Monsieur Delacourt nods at Oncle Gérard, not even saying thank you to Pascal.

"I'd like to show you a filly foal, just a week old, one of his first crop," Oncle Gérard says, and the two men walk slowly up the yard.

"What an awful man!" Cass nearly explodes when they are out of earshot. "Treating you like a servant! Didn't you mind?"

Pascal grins, unfastening the stallion's bridle. "You

noticed? No, it doesn't really bother me. Horse people are very old-fashioned. He could have offered me a tip – that would have been worse. You'd better go after them in case they want the foal led out. I don't see why you shouldn't be a servant too."

Cass goes, but the men are looking at the foal over the half-door and don't require her services. She listens to Monsieur Delacourt with distaste as he holds forth about bloodlines. She feels the slight more on Pascal's behalf than she would for herself.

Two days later, on a misty, drizzly evening, Cass has gone up to her flat after work and is about to have a shower when she hears Pascal shouting her name from the yard. He has only just left for home, a few minutes earlier. Throwing on a shirt, she goes to her bedroom window and opens it.

"Can you come and help?" Pascal calls up. "I think the yearlings are out!"

"I'm coming. Two minutes." She pulls her dirty jeans back on, snatches up her waterproof and runs downstairs. Pascal is getting tools out of the store. He hands her a hammer and a cardboard box of nails and staples, and shoulders some stakes and lengths of rail.

"I noticed a weak rail yesterday. I meant to do something about it. Can you fetch a bucket of oats and three head-collars?"

"Where have they gone, the yearlings?"

"I think they must have got into the reserve. They shouldn't come to any harm there, as long as they don't get out to the road."

Together, they hurry across the mares' field and clamber through the fence into the lush meadow where the yearlings have been grazing. It is bordered by the belt of woodland that forms a boundary to the bird reserve. Cass sees the gap as they approach – a rail has splintered and is sagging to the ground in two halves. Beyond, the damp grass is trodden down, showing the yearlings' escape route.

Pascal swears under his breath. "It's my fault. I should have known they'd find that weak place." He dumps his fencing materials to one side of the gap and steps over the lower rail. "God knows where they've got to. It's a big area in here."

Cass follows him through wet grass, saplings and bluebells to the edge of the lake. It feels odd to come here with someone else, especially Pascal. It has become her own private place, her dream place.

He stops at the shore.

"This way." She points to a hoofprint on the muddy path. "They've gone towards the cottage."

He turns round to face her, his face puzzled. "Why do you say that?"

"They have. That's where they are."

Pascal hesitates, then walks on, his boots squelching. Cass senses his reluctance to go that way. The drizzle falls with a steady, hypnotic sound, spattering on the lake, dripping from the leaves. The air is hazy with moisture, blurring the emerging greens of the trees across the lake. Neither of them speaks. The strange, cut-off atmosphere of the reserve creeps over Cass and she knows that Pascal feels it too. When he looks round to check that she's still following his face is set, lips compressed.

He stops by the inlet where the path continues round to the hide, scanning the track for hoofprints. Cass goes on ahead of him towards the cottage. There is a tight, choky feeling in her throat. The undergrowth is thicker than ever, dense and lush, soaking her legs. Regardless of brambles tearing at her jeans, she walks on steadily, pulled to the cottage.

The damp air hangs around the building. Its windows are blank, like hollow eye sockets.

She must hide, quickly, before someone sees her. They have told her that she must always keep quiet, must never wander about in the open, otherwise they will all be taken away and never come back. Sometimes, when they are sure there's no one around, she is allowed to play outside, but only in the orchard, never by the lake, and never, never out of sight of the house. Once or twice, very daring, she has been as far as the lake to look at the birds there, but she's never told them that. They would scold her and not let her out at all.

What will happen if someone comes here to find them? Someone, that is, apart from Madame Duclos who comes every day, giving a special call so that they will know it's safe. If someone else comes, Maman says, they must hide. They must get into the space between the two bedrooms and keep very quiet. It will be like a game, Maman says, keeping very quiet for as long as they can. Not even a sneeze will be allowed.

But someone is following her now. She hasn't been careful enough. It's happening. She is being followed and it is all her fault, for not doing as she was told. They will all be found and taken away, unless she goes somewhere else, not to the cottage at all. Like a bird pretending to be injured and leading a pursuer away from her nest. She veers away and runs, pushing through wet screens of hawthorn, ducking under branches. A twig cracks under her foot like a rifle shot; she is no good at hiding, no good at all. The man is coming after her, shouting something. She won't turn round. The trees are fighting her now, they are on his side, reaching out wet thorny branches to hold her back. Her lungs are bursting, burning, her throat dry: she isn't used to running, staying in the house all the time. The man is running too. Faster and fitter, he will catch her, but she won't tell him where she has come from and then the others will be safe. But she isn't captured yet. She raised her hands to push the branches aside, to find a small place where she can fit and he can't. She can hear his breathing as he closes on her, like a fox closing on a rabbit, or a hound on a deer. All sense of purpose is lost in the blindness of panic. Turning, she defies him, her eyes hot with fear.

"No!" she yells.

"Cass! Cass!"

His arms close around her. She struggles in his grasp, freeing an arm and hitting him in the face. Cass? Is that someone's name, or a command in his own language?

He winces from the blow, and then gives her a little shake. "Cass! It's all right – Cass!"

She is too exhausted to struggle any more. His arms are tight around her, too strong for escape. Slowly, her eyes focus, recognizing. It is Pascal she has been running away from; she can't remember why, only the sense of terror that possessed her. His eyes are fixed on her face, baffled, appalled. He loosens his grip, holding her lightly by the arms.

"Cass, what's wrong? Why did you run off like that?"

"I don't know. I –"

"You looked as if you'd seen a – your face just then, you looked like someone else –"

"I – it's a sort of dream, a nightmare. I can't remember it now."

He must think she is going mad. She thinks so herself.

"A nightmare? Now?"

"Yes – it's this place. The atmosphere here. Something happened here. Can you feel it?" She looks at him closely, pleading. "You can, can't you?"

"Yes. Yes, I can."

She sags with relief. Pascal *knows*; she could tell, back there in the woods, as they approached the cottage. And that means she isn't mad. She isn't the only one.

"But only because –" Pascal begins, then checks himself. "Not like you."

"But you *must* –" Cass gives up, too bewildered to continue. She remembers why they're here. It is twilight, the colours fading; it will be dark soon. "The horses! We still haven't found them!"

Pascal looks at her doubtfully. "Are you sure you're all right?"

"Yes. As soon as we get away from here."

They push their way back through the hawthorns towards the path and find the bucket and headcollars where Cass dropped them, by the path. Pascal scoops up most of the oats in his hands and Cass gathers up the headcollars, looping the ropes over her arm, relieved to be doing something practical. She is trembling, aware that Pascal must think she's off her head. Her vision has gone now as abruptly as it came. When she hears snapping twigs in the orchard she looks in that direction without fear. One of the yearlings is pushing between the trees, looking mildly surprised. It surrenders easily for a handful of oats. Pascal gives the rope to Cass and walks round to the back of the cottage, appearing shortly with the other two yearlings caught and submissive.

He looks at Cass oddly. "You said they'd be at the cottage."

"Yes."

In the growing gloom they find their way back through the gap, coaxing the young horses over the lower rail and then releasing them.

"It's too dark to do much now," Pascal says. "I'll just fix a rail across and leave it till tomorrow to do a better job."

He lifts a rail and positions it across the gap. Cass holds one end in place, watching Pascal's hands as he works, looking at his bent head and his thick hair, his brows lowered in concentration. It hurts her to look at him. Why did she run away? Who did she think he was? She can remember only the blind sense of panic, not the reason for it.

It is dark by the time they return to the yard. Pascal turns on the outside lights and stows his tools in the store, and Cass goes into the harness-room with the headcollars and then locks up.

"God, it's late," Pascal says. He puts a hand on her shoulder and looks at her closely. "Will you be all right now? Should I take you up to your uncle's house? I don't think I ought to leave you on your own, after –"

His hand is heavy on her shoulder, holding her, its warmth

burning her damp shirt, burning through her whole body. She
will cry if he carries on looking at her like that.

"Don't leave me, then," she whispers. "Stay."

What is she saying? Someone braver and bolder has taken
over her voice.

"You know I can't –" But even while he is saying it, his
arms are closing round her and hers round him. His body is
slim and strong, smelling of wet denim and horse. His mouth
is against her ear, whispering "Cass, Cass!", his breath a
caress. Something is stirring and leaping inside her. She turns
her face and his mouth meets hers, hesitant and then firm. His
arms tighten and then, abruptly, he releases his grip and steps
back to stare at her, his eyes wide and horrified.

"God, what am I doing?" He looks away from her, deliberately withdrawing. "Cass, you must go upstairs now and I
must go home. Unless you want me to go up to the house with
you first." He is not quite in control of his voice.

"I'm sorry, I didn't mean –"

She knows it's a lie. She did mean.

Pascal hesitates. 'Will you be all right now?"

"Yes."

"Are you sure? You don't want me to fetch your aunt?"

"No!" Cass shakes her head vehemently.

"There are people in the flat next door, aren't there, if
you're – ill, or anything?"

"It's all right. I'm not ill."

At the door to her stairs, he leans towards her and kisses her
cheek. It is a chaste kiss, not like the first one; the sort of kiss a
brother might give, or an uncle. It is a gesture of affection, a
way of putting their relationship back within proper bound-

aries. Cass can't look at him. He turns off the yard lights and opens her door.

"Goodnight, Cass. Take care."

"Goodnight. I'm sorry."

Pascal almost shoves her inside and then walks away quickly. Upstairs, without turning on the light, Cass looks out of her bedroom window. She hears his car door slam but there is no sound of the engine starting. He must be sitting there in the darkness. What is he thinking? From the confusion of her thoughts she sends out a silent, desperate message: *Pascal, I love you.* She is disturbed by his distress, aroused, frightened, ashamed, all at once, still aware of the feel of him, his smell and taste. After a few minutes the engine ignites and gains strength and the headlights flash up, sharply illuminating grass stems and hedgerow. The tyres bite as the car reverses quickly and then pulls away. He is gone. The silence of the night settles around her.

She mustn't love Pascal. It is hopeless. Suddenly exhausted by her emotions, she throws herself face down on her bed. From a deep spring of grief inside her the tears rise up, spilling, burning.

12. Chez Maurice

In the morning, Cass feeds all the horses and sweeps the yard before Pascal arrives. She wants to be purposefully occupied, and there is no shortage of jobs: Oncle Gérard has asked her to put out bedding plants this morning and all the lawns need mowing. She hears Pascal's car arriving and sees him leading the stallion out, but does not speak to him until he walks across the damp lawn to find her in the garden outhouse where she is trying to get the petrol mower started.

"How are you feeling today?" he asks. "Did you sleep all right?"

She nods, concentrating on the mower.

"No more nightmares?"

"No," Cass says.

"I'm sorry," Pascal says carefully, "about last night. I shouldn't have done what I did." He is digging the heel of his boot into the grass, scuffing up moss.

"It was my fault," Cass says. "Not yours. I should be the one to apologize." She bends down and tugs at the starter cable. Nothing happens.

"Well – both of us," Pascal concedes. "You were upset and I was worried. But I'm not trying to make excuses."

"I know."

"The point is that I – well, I didn't mean – I love my wife and I wouldn't want you to think –"

"No. I don't."

She is acting with a control she doesn't really possess.

Pascal looks relieved, and says, "So it's all right then?"

"Yes, it's all right." She smiles hesitantly and Pascal smiles back, looking at her directly for the first time. Another tug at the cable sends the mower sputtering into life, stinking of petrol and fumes, drowning any further conversation. Pascal walks back across the grass and she watches him go, fighting an urge to run after him and say *No, it's not all right. I love you. I know it's awful but I can't help it...*

When he has gone out of sight behind the stable block, she starts to mow. The cut grass flies up in a green wave, smelling of summer. Should she leave, she wonders: tell her aunt and uncle that she's decided to go home? It would be clean and decisive – like an amputation without an anaesthetic – but at least final. Even before she has fully realized it as an option, she knows she won't do it. There is more than Pascal to hold her here. Her weird vision at the cottage seems to confirm that she has been brought here for some reason to discover what happened during the war. She *must* find out. She can't love Pascal but she can do that.

Pascal knows more than he will tell her, but now she has made it difficult, if not impossible, to ask. He feels the powerful atmosphere that hangs around the cottage, just as she does. "But only because –" he said, when she asked him. Because he knows what happened there, she thinks he meant. But she can't ask him without referring to her behaviour last night, a subject best left undiscussed.

She spends the whole day brooding unhappily.

Only next morning does it occur to her that there is at least one person willing to speak freely about the past – Maurice's wife. Under the pretext of asking how he's recovering, she drives into St Privat before lunch, parks her car in the square and goes into the *Intermarché* to buy grapes and a bottle of wine for Maurice. The village is as quiet and shuttered as usual, but there's one house at least where she knows she will be received and welcomed. Maurice, much improved, is out in the garden with the newspaper while his wife Yvonne prepares a casserole in the kitchen. Cass seizes her chance. When Madame Lepin offers her a glass of cider she sits at the kitchen table instead of joining Maurice outside. She likes the Lepins' kitchen: dark-panelled in wood, traditional, with brass-bottomed saucepans hanging from a dresser, jars of herbs, flour, coffee.

"How much longer do you think Maurice will be off work?" she asks casually.

"I'm not sure he'll be going back at all," Madame Lepin says, briskly chopping onions and garlic. "It's hard work for a man his age – not too bad at this time of year, but worse when winter comes. And awkward hours. Apparently Pascal Duclos likes the work and it suits him at present, so he's happy to stay on."

Cass tries not to show her relief. She shouldn't *be* relieved – things would be easier all round if Maurice came back and Pascal left, although a lot less interesting. Madame Lepin hasn't noticed. She seems to accept Cass without curiosity, glad of someone to talk to while she works.

"Pascal's lent me a pair of binoculars," Cass remarks, "and I've been in the reserve a few times. You know that derelict cottage in there, at the far end? I was wondering why someone doesn't fix it up and live there. It'd be a nice place for someone to live."

Madame Lepin stops chopping for a moment to look at

Cass before her big knife resumes its rhythm, leaving neat slices of onion on the board. Cass wonders why she doesn't cry. Cass can't cut up onions without crying.

"The Jews' house, you mean?"

There it is, as simply as that. Cass's head reels with the implications. "It belonged to Jewish people? In the war?"

"No, it didn't belong to them. It belonged to your great-grandfather, although no one had used it for a long time. It was already empty before the war. Hidden as it was in those dense woods – even thicker then, with the shooting lake left to grow wild – it was used by the Resistance, to hide people they wanted to keep hidden. Aircrew, usually, till they were fit enough to be passed on down the line and get back to England. A risky business. They had to go all the way down to Portugal. Gaston Duclos – you know, Pascal's grandfather, who was here the other day – and *his* father used to forge papers for them."

"But the Jews. Where did they come from?"

"From Caen originally, I think. There were rumours. They'd been in hiding since the Germans started the deportations. First in someone's attic, then when that got too risky they were moved on here. By another Resistance unit, I think." She frowns with the effort of remembering.

"How did they stay hidden?"

"They had to. Marie Duclos – that was Gaston's mother – used to slip in and out with food whenever she could. Fuel in winter, though they had to be careful about smoke. Risky, with the Germans so close. There were soldiers billeted in your aunt and uncle's house, did you know that?"

Cass nods. Her heart is pounding. "What happened to them? The Jewish family?"

"They were discovered. They were sent to Drancy, that camp in Paris, and then on to Auschwitz. So people say. That awful journey all the way across Germany and into Poland. Days, it took, crammed into railway trucks. And Auschwitz at the end of it."

"And they died there?" Cass whispers.

"As far as anyone knows. It was about a year before the concentration camps were liberated. I doubt they survived."

Cass is staring at her hands clasping the cider glass on the table. They are the only still points in whirling confusion. If she doesn't hold on she will lose her balance and spin with the vortex inside her head, sucked down, dragged into blackness. She has known, all the time, that something dreadful happened to the nowhere girl. She has *been* the nowhere girl, felt her loneliness and panic, her incomprehension. They died, all of them. She knows they died. In that terrible place with the high wire fences and the gas chambers and the ovens, where human beings were stripped into piles of hair and gold teeth, became wisps of smoke from the incinerators. The nowhere girl is truly nowhere.

Madame Lepin glances at Cass. "That's why no one wanted to live in the cottage afterwards, to answer your question. No one local, anyway. Outsiders wouldn't know."

But Cass knew. And the whole story is here, in this kitchen, in Madame Lepin's head. If only she can ask the right questions.

"Was that why my great-grandfather shot himself?" she asks. "Because the Jewish family had been betrayed?"

"I really don't know. I was only a child, about nine or ten

No one spoke much about your great-grandfather's death, not that I can remember. It was hushed up. The war was nearly at an end then, after the Liberation – we could see an end to it all."

"Who found him? My great-aunt?"

"No." Madame Lepin tips the onions and garlic into a casserole dish, pours oil in and starts to cube meat, turning it in deft hands, frowning. "No. She went away, I remember. Just before the Liberation. And she only came back after he shot himself. It was her house then, of course. There being no sons, and her the oldest of the daughters."

"My aunt went away? Why?"

"I don't know that. I just remember she went away suddenly."

"By why would she? Where would she go?"

"I don't know. Why don't you ask her?" Madame Lepin says.

"Smells good, Yvonne." Maurice appears in the doorway, bracing his arms against the frame. "So how's that new foal coming on, Cass?" He pours himself a glass of cider and sits down at the table. Cass knows that Madame Lepin won't talk so freely in front of him; the conversation is over.

"That black mare's in season. I was afraid she was going to be," Pascal tells Cass that evening. "She'll have to be covered again."

"What do you mean, covered?" Cass asks, thinking it's some veterinary procedure.

"You know," Pascal says shortly. "Put to the stallion. We'd better do it this evening, when we've finished."

Cass is cleaning headcollars. "We? Don't they do it by themselves?"

Pascal's mouth twitches, not quite a smile; he avoids looking at her directly. "Of course they know how to. But it's not usual with such valuable animals just to turn them out in a field together. They might kick or injure each other. You'll have to handle the mare and I'll take Mistral."

He explains what Cass must do to get the mare ready and what will happen when they take the two horses out to the paddock, how they must minimize the risk to the horses and themselves. Cass listens, dismayed by the ritual which is about to take place and her own part in it. She is so ignorant about horses. She thought it just happened, out in the field at night when no one's watching.

"The mare won't be any trouble," Pascal says. "She's - strongly in season."

Cass guesses that to another man he would have used a more direct phrase. She goes to fetch the mare in from the paddock and sees what he means: the mare is standing by the fence, gazing across at the stallion, taut and quivering. She hardly notices Cass approaching and putting the headcollar on her. In the stable, Cass buckles felt boots to the mare's hind feet, a precaution in case she resists the stallion and kicks out at him, although that doesn't seem likely. The black mare is still looking for him, straining at the door, her whole body shaken by deep, throaty whinneys. From the other end of the yard, the stallion's imperious neighing answers her. Cass changes the headcollar for a bridle and leads the mare out to the small paddock to wait for Pascal and the stallion.

Mistral comes across the yard, prancing, restrained by Pascal. He is beautiful in his male conceit, his neck arched to the bit, his ears pricked sharply, nostrils flaring, like a warhorse. He calls to the mare and she answers excitedly, turning her head to look at him as he comes through the paddock gate, high-stepping. Cass positions the mare as Pascal has told her and he brings the stallion up from behind, at an angle, so that the mare can see him and won't kick out. Mistral approaches in a series of sideways leaps, controlled by Pascal, and then he is behind the mare, snorting, rearing up, his hooves flailing. Cass is startled, reminded of her fear when the stallion struck at her, but the mare doesn't budge. Mistral steadies himself, forelegs straddling the mare's shoulders. He is whickering, deep, vibrating tremors through widely flared nostrils, like the mare. It is all over quickly. The stallion's body is taut as he thrusts and then his head sags, all the vibrant energy gone out of him. It is brutally abrupt, yet not without tenderness. He disengages himself from the mare and Pascal leads him away.

Cass pats the mare's neck and takes her back to the stable. The mare is quiet now. Cass feels shaken and moved by what she has seen, the brute simplicity of the two animals coming together, black mare and grey stallion. In spite of the bridles, the felt boots, the restraint, in those few moments the two horses weren't tamed and domesticated, someone's property, but wild creatures, driven by the strength of their instincts. This brief, supervised coupling should result in a thoroughbred foal next spring. It is a financial arrangement, Cass knows: the mare's owner has paid for the stallion's sperm, his bloodline. Both horses are valuable gene banks, breeding materials. The mating was an incongruous meeting of commercial interest and the pure, elemental forces of nature.

Cass turns the black mare out in the field with the others, where she immediately starts grazing as if the drama of the last few minutes is already forgotten. Work is finished now for the evening. Cass doesn't want to come face to face with Pascal, not just yet, but he comes in with the stallion's bridle while she is in the harness-room and runs water at the sink to rinse the bit.

"That was all right," he says, very businesslike. "She might have to be covered again tomorrow though. It'll be easier next time."

Easier for Cass and himself, he means; for the horses it was straightforward enough. She can tell that he is as deeply embarrassed as she is by the respective roles they have had to take.

The Jewish family. Auschwitz. Cass's new knowledge is something black and poisonous. She has tried to bury it in the back of her mind but now it seeps out like toxic waste, polluting everything she thinks and sees and does. She can no longer look out of her bedroom window without knowing that the trees at the edge of the reserve, delicate in their new foliage and full of birdsong, shield the house where the nowhere girl and her family lived in terror. Every day a day survived. Every tomorrow full of fresh dangers. Dependent on the woman from the village with her baskets of food and fuel. Unable to light fires in winter, because of the smoke above the trees. In constant fear of German voices by the lake, a stray soldier taking an evening walk in the woods. The parents trying to explain to the children why they must never laugh, shout, run freely outside, play like other children. Why they must live nowhere.

Cass feels as if something has reached out from the past to touch her, to pull her back. She feels as if she is both victim and persecutor. She knew already about the deportations from France, the extermination camps; she knew the facts. But this is different, knowing that it happened here. The nowhere girl, who has walked the same paths as Cass and breathed the same air, whose voice Cass knows and whose skin she has inhabited, was captured here. She was put on a train, in a cattle-truck, and sent away to die. Her life was of less account than the horses grazing in the meadows outside, less valuable than the cells splitting into life inside the black mare. The nowhere girl has spoken to Cass, called to her. Summoned her.

What did Tante Eugénie have to do with it? That part of the story is still incomplete. Did Tante Eugénie betray the Jewish family to her German boyfriend? But why should she? And perhaps no one betrayed them – it wouldn't have been impossible, surely, for the Germans to hear or see something, or to have Marie from the village tracked on one of her visits.

Marie Duclos. Gaston's mother. That makes her, Cass realizes, Pascal's great-grandmother. His own family tried to save the Jewish refugees, but failed. Pascal knows that. What else does he know, if only he would tell her?

Cass looks out over the darkling fields, shivers, and pulls her curtains, shutting out the night.

13. Chez Pascal

"We would like it," Pascal says, "if you would come over for a meal on Saturday evening."

Cass has just made coffee and they are sitting in the yard to drink it, Cass on a bale of hay, Pascal on an upturned bucket. She looks at him, noting the careful *we*.

"Really?"

Pascal nods. "I'd like you to meet Monique. And Gilles."

Cass doesn't know what to say, torn between a curiosity to see Pascal at home with his wife and child, and the certain knowledge that she will find it difficult. How much does Monique know about her? What has Pascal said? Has he told Monique everything, about embracing her, kissing her? They are sitting just a few yards away from the place where it happened. Cass feels as if the intensity of that moment should have burned itself into the stones, as it has in her memory. It will never happen again, she knows, because Pascal has no intention of letting it.

"Please come," Pascal says. "You're too lonely here."

"Oh, if it's just a favour –" Cass retorts. She pulls a stem of hay from the bale, peevishly, and twists it round her finger.

"It's not a favour. I want you to come."

"Why?"

It sounds more belligerent than she intends. Pascal's brows contract. "All right, forget it. Don't come if you don't want to. Just an idea."

"No, sorry." She is contrite at once. "I didn't mean to be rude. I *would* like to come. Thank you."

She was never seriously going to refuse; she would do anything Pascal asked.

They finish their coffee and she goes back to weeding Tante Eugénie's herbaceous border, yanking out goose grass and creeping buttercup. She thinks she understands why Pascal has invited her, even though it will probably be difficult for him too. Introducing her into his home is a way, perhaps, of showing that he is out of bounds; but it also shows that he wants to be friendly and that she is accepted. He doesn't blame her for what happened, though he easily could. She decides that he must have told Monique, because he is basically honest; he has proved that.

Is she as honest herself? If Pascal had accepted her rash offer that night and gone upstairs with her, would she have said: "Oh no, Pascal. You must go home. This is wrong."?

No.

What would she do now, this minute, if he came across the lawn and put his arms round her and kissed her in the way she only has to remember for sparks to start leaping? Would she say, "Stop it, Pascal. Go back to your work," and push him away?

No. She doesn't have the strength of will. Yet she knows that she would not respect him as she does if he were willing to have a furtive relationship with her. That must mean she respects him more than she respects herself.

She frowns, prodding at an obstinate root with her trowel. Was that how it was for Tante Eugénie and her German soldier? Nothing mattered except being together?

Nationality, loyalty, morality, resistance, all the things she was supposed to care about, dissolved into meaningless concepts when set against the urge to be with someone she loved?

Cass disentangles a mat of goose grass. She realizes that she doesn't *know* any of this; it is only speculation, though the image of a smiling blond German in uniform is strong in her mind. And even if Tante Eugénie did have a German boyfriend, that doesn't mean she told him about the Jewish family. What would she have to gain by that?

She jumps, biting her lip, at the sound of a voice behind her. "You're doing a good job there, Cécile dear." It is Tante Eugénie herself, walking along the edge of lawn from the house, rather unsteady in the heeled court shoes she always wears. She bends stiffly to tweak off a dead end of twig. "Another two or three weeks and this border will be at its best."

She is well wrapped-up in a high-necked blouse and long cardigan, even though it isn't at all cold.

"You're not bored here, are you, Cécile?" she asks. "There's very little here to amuse a young person. I'm afraid it's rather dull for you. You must be missing your friends at home."

Cass hasn't given her friends, or Robbie, a single thought for some time. She squints up from her kneeling position. "Oh, no. It's not dull at all. I like it here."

Tante Eugénie's anxious expression gives way to a smile of relief. "Don't work too hard, will you, dear? I don't want you getting ill again."

I'd have to be pretty feeble to be exhausted by a bit of light gardening, Cass thinks, but she smiles and says, "I'm perfectly all right now, honestly."

"As long as you're sure. Those horses take up a lot of your time, I know. Late nights."

"I don't mind at all."

Tante Eugénie continues walking along the border, holding her hand out to touch a peony bud, exclaiming to herself at a new discovery. Cass notices how frail she looks: an old lady, venturing out in the spring sunshine to look at her plants. Harmless, kind, in her rather austere way. Cass feels guilty about the sensational theories she has been inventing.

All day Saturday, she feels very anxious about going to Pascal's house in the evening. Pascal leaves at his usual time after sketching her a map, and she goes upstairs to shower and change. At the last minute she nearly loses her nerve, deciding to phone Pascal and make an excuse. She dithers by the harness-room phone, picking up the receiver and replacing it three times before locking up again and going out to her car. Anyway, Pascal would know she'd chickened out.

She follows his directions carefully and parks in the road outside. Villeneuve is a much larger place than St Privat, town rather than village, with several shops and a square surrounded by pollarded plane trees. The sketch map directs her to a quiet road on the edge of town. The house is small, in a terraced row, built of grey stone with a tiled roof. There are pots of tulips in the walled front garden. Two cars are parked in the driveway: Pascal's black Renault and a white Peugeot, which she recognizes from its numberplate as the one she saw parked by the bird reserve. Odd. Pascal didn't mention anyone else coming, or the fact that he knows the invisible birdwatcher. She doesn't hurry to go in, leaning across to look at her reflection in the driving mirror and tidying her hair. Her throat feels dry and she wishes she hadn't come.

Pascal opens the door to her. "You look different," he says, in reference to the long skirt and soft cream shirt she is wearing, and leads her through an interior doorway whose frame is so low that he has to duck. In a low-ceilinged room with an open staircase, a young man sits at a table drinking wine and watching a baby stacking bricks on the tiled floor.

"Cass, this is Philippe," Pascal says. "And this is Gilles." He scoops up the baby, who gazes at Cass with round blue eyes and a worried expression. "And this is Monique," Pascal adds as someone comes through from the kitchen. "Monique, Cass."

At that point Gilles starts to cry. Monique throws up her hands and smiles at Cass, Pascal tries to calm the baby and Philippe picks up a rattle from the floor and shakes it.

"Excellent timing. Welcome to our peaceful home," Monique says to Cass as the baby's yells grow louder.

"It must be me. It only took one look to set him off," Cass says.

Monique is small and dark, rather as Cass imagined her, with shining straight hair parted on one side and falling to chin length; she wears a striped T-shirt and baggy trousers and looks quite young, not more than twenty or so. Cass hands over the bottle of Sauvignon she has brought. Relieved that Monique isn't stunningly chic or formidable, Cass is prepared to like her. Monique isn't really pretty until she smiles, and then her face is transformed by an open, slightly mischievous smile without a hint of suspicion or resentment. Cass already feels more at ease than she expected. Delicious warm smells waft through from the kitchen, flavoured with herbs. The main room they are in is comfortable, rather cluttered, with an overflowing bookcase and a lot of trailing plants. Pascal, failing to pacify the baby, carries him out through patio doors into a walled garden.

"I'm glad you could come," Monique says. "Have you met Philippe?"

"No, but she's got my binoculars," Philippe says. "I hope they're useful."

"Oh, they're yours!" Cass says. "I didn't know."

"Philippe is Pascal's brother," Monique explains. "He lives in Bayeux, so we see each other quite often. Let me get you some wine."

Surprised, Cass looks at Philippe; she didn't know Pascal had a brother. She notes the resemblance: not immediately obvious, but there in the dark brows and blue eyes, and the strong jaw-line.

"I've seen your car at the reserve a couple of times," she tells him.

"Yes, I go there two or three times each week. There's another one near Bénouville, if you're interested."

"Don't you want your binoculars back?"

"No, you can hang on to them. They're my spare pair."

Monique hands Cass a glass of white wine and tops up Philippe's glass. Outside, Cass can see Pascal walking up and down slowly with the baby in his arms.

"I'm sorry he's grumpy," Monique says. "It's a bit late for

him. He's usually in bed by now and he gets irritable when he's tired. He's normally quite good-natured."

"The baby, she means, not Pascal," Philippe jokes.

Soon Pascal comes back in and says he is taking Gilles up to bed. The other three drink wine and talk, with Monique occasionally darting into the kitchen to prod or stir something.

"Where do you keep the equipment for the printing business?" Cass asks her, having vaguely expected it to be in a building attached to the house. Outside there is just a garden with high stone walls, a lilac in full flower and more planted tubs.

"In a lock-up shed two doors along, behind the *boulangerie*. It's nothing very grand. We just about manage to keep going," Monique says. "Now that Pascal's working with your uncle, I do a few hours in the morning and he takes over in the afternoons."

Philippe does most of the talking, telling them a lot of funny anecdotes about his work – he is a reporter on a local newspaper, Cass gathers – and the eccentricities of his colleagues. His presence is an asset, ensuring that there are no awkward gaps in the conversation. By the time Pascal comes down again, Monique is ready to serve the meal. It is informal: *rillettes*, a *gougère* with salad and potatoes, lots of wine. Interested in the talk and the company, Cass forgets to feel embarrassed. The similarity between the brothers is superficial, she decides: Philippe, probably two or three years younger, is the more outgoing of the two – sharper, more self-aware, and, she guesses, more ambitious. His blue eyes, so like Pascal's, gleam with enjoyment as he talks. He has a way of making an everyday incident into a mini-drama, relishing his choice of phrase, his skilled impersonations. He is smaller and darker than Pascal, more obviously good-looking, in a way that reminds Cass uncomfortably of Kelvin. Pascal seems different too: relaxed, laughing, prompting his brother's performance with timely questions. He is wearing a white linen shirt, which suits him, with sleeves rolled up. Between them, he and Monique ensure that Cass isn't left out of the conversation. She tries not to let her eyes follow Pascal when he gets up to fetch more wine, clear the plates or run upstairs to check the baby. She is acutely aware of all that she finds most attractive in him: his quiet attentiveness, the intelligent gleam in his eyes, the way his upper lip lifts over his teeth when he smiles. But she is aware too of the unspoken communication between him and Monique – a quick glance to signal that the baby needs attention, a touch of hands as they pass close to each other. She is relieved to find herself liking Pascal's wife, but seeing them together makes her realize that she has been incredibly foolish. She has made something momentous out of what was, for Pascal, a spontaneous impulse, instantly regretted.

"What do you do on your days off, Cass?" Philippe asks her, passing the cheese plate.

"Oh – nothing much. Sightseeing, being a tourist. I spent a day in Bayeux and I've been to Omaha Beach."

"Must be a bit lonely, though, stuck out there in that dozy village miles from anywhere. It'd drive me mad."

Trying not to look at Pascal, Cass doesn't answer. Perhaps it *is* driving her mad.

"You ought to go out more," Philippe continues. "I've got

lots of friends in Bayeux and Caen. There are always parties and things going on. Why don't you come along some time?"

Cass's eyes meet Monique's across the table. She wonders briefly and a little resentfully, whether Pascal has engineered this as a diversion. A consolation prize.

14. Dissolving

Her own voice startles her as she screams. It's a high-pitched squeal of terror, not quite her own, that frightens her still more, but she can't help it, after so long being told to keep quiet, not to laugh or shout. The tension of all the months in hiding is streaming out of her mouth in a long, drawn-out wail.

"Hush! Hush!" Her mother is trying to soothe her. But Maman can't put this right, can't hug and comfort her and shut out the nasty brutish world. The outside world has broken in on them. Their own nowhere world is broken open and exposed to the sneering glances of the soldiers. Maman's hands are tied behind her back and there is a spreading bruise on her face where one of the soldiers hit her. Papa has already been led away, into the woods. He gave a last despairing look as he went as if he never expected to see her or Maman again. And then the soldier cuffed the side of his head and prodded him in the back with his gun to make him walk out into the woods, where the new leaves are tender and green and the treetops full of birdsong. Maman flew at one of the soldiers, hands outstretched like claws, and he hit her so hard that she fell back against the wall. And then tied her hands so that she couldn't hit out again.

The cottage can't save them now, the cottage they have made into a home. Father brought the *mezuzah* from their old home, with its parchment prayer, and pinned it to the right-hand side of the doorpost, where he touches it every time he passes through, and mutters a prayer: *May he who makes peace in the highest grant peace to us*... But prayers can't save them now. God can't save them. No one can save them from these cruel, triumphant intruders. The toys brought from home are scattered over the floor, broken, trodden by the soldiers' boots. The soldiers have smashed the windows and ripped down the curtains Maman has sewn so patiently through the long evenings, blackout curtains to stop any gleam of candlelight from showing outside. One of them ripped the *mezuzah* from the doorpost, laughing as he ground it underfoot. The soldiers have destroyed the home made from nothing. They are taking away the life salvaged from ruins.

A soldier says something harshly in his own language. Another prods Maman in the back. She flashes him a look of pride and contempt, getting another vicious jab in return. They are all leaving now, pushed out into the sunshine.

Her screams have died down to sobbing whimpers, as if she is trying to comfort herself. Following her mother – who walks with dignity despite her tied hands, her stockingless legs, bare feet in shoes so old they are tied together with string – she stumbles along the path, through the orchard, past the thicket where the nightingale sings.

Cass floats slowly into a pool of darkness. The sobs echo inside her head, pressing silently her eardrums. The blackness is there in the room, tingling, touching her face and her arms with prickles of fear. She fumbles for the light switch and with one click the shadows leap away. She stares at her room: flowered curtains, wardrobe, her black jeans draped over a chair. It is all too bright, as if it might crack and disintegrate. Underneath, the blackness is still waiting.

It's two-fifteen in the morning, silent and cold. She pushes back the duvet and goes into the kitchen, turning on the light. The window is black and glassy and she is suddenly terrified that she will see the nowhere girl's face looking in at her, or the bruised, suffering face of the mother.

If she goes back to sleep, she will go with them. She will be taken away in a truck and be swallowed up with the thousands of faceless dead and become a wisp of smoke from an incinerator, dissolving in the air.

Why shouldn't she? Would it make any difference, one more? Would anyone notice?

It feels like an act of enormous courage to cross the kitchen floor and pull down the blind. Deliberately, she thinks of the people in the holiday flat next door, newly-arrived today: a meek-looking couple with a sulky twelve-year-old son. She has only spoken to them briefly but they are her anchor to sanity. She pictures them lying neatly in their beds, untroubled by black dreams. If she's desperate she can knock on their door.

She controls her trembling enough to boil a kettle and make herself a mug of tea. Why doesn't she leave, go home to school and friends and sanity? She could pack her bags now and be gone by morning.

But she knows she can't. There is something holding her here, a powerful magnetic tug. Her fear is bringing her closer, not driving her away.

"I enjoyed it last night," she says to Pascal in the morning. "Thank you for inviting me."

"Good. We enjoyed it too. I hope you'll come again."

They are in the mare and foal's stable. Pascal is getting the foal used to being handled: brushing it, picking up its feet and tapping them so that it won't be frightened of being shod later. Everything seems normal today: the sun is warm enough for the mare and foal to spend a few hours in the paddock, and house martins are swooping into the stable eaves. It is more like summer than spring. Cass releases the mare and watches her go down the field through the buttercups, the mare ambling, the foal skipping and bucking, stopping to stare amazed at a white butterfly. Beyond are the trees of the nature reserve, innocuous in the sunshine.

"I know about the Jewish people in the cottage," she says suddenly to Pascal.

"Yes." He looks in that direction. "I thought you'd find out. I wish you hadn't." As he turns away from the gate, she glimpses his expression – bitter, shuttered. But he adds, "It's an awful place, that house. It should have been knocked down years ago."

Later that week, about to start the evening feeds, Cass hears a car pull up at the yard gate and comes out of the feed room to see Philippe getting out of his white car. He waves when he sees her and she goes over to say hello.

"Have you come to see Pascal? He's gone out to check the yearlings. He'll be back in a minute."

"OK. I'll hang on then. Actually, it was you I came to see." Philippe grins at her. "Do you fancy an hour of bird-watching?" He has his binoculars slung round his neck.

"Well – I haven't quite finished."

"I don't mind waiting," Philippe says. "I've got a report to write." He is leaning against the fence, not much bothered whether she accepts or not. He gives the impression of being totally at ease with himself.

Pascal is coming down the field, surprised to see his brother. Philippe explains, and Pascal says, "You go, Cass, if you want to. I'll finish off here. There's only the feeds and hay to do."

"Do you want to come too?" Cass asks, but Pascal shakes his head.

"I've got to get back. Monique goes swimming tonight and it's my turn to have Gilles."

"Family duties call, *hein*?" Philippe says.

Cass goes upstairs to fetch her binoculars. They say goodbye to Pascal and walk down to the reserve entrance. Cass is not sure why she agreed to come; she hasn't been to the reserve lately and she's not sure she wants to go there now. Certainly not to the cottage.

"I'm not sure about this place," she remarks. "I've been here on my own a few times and it gives me the creeps."

Putting it mildly.

Philippe nods. "Too many ghosts?"

He says it lightly, almost flippantly, but as if he knows. Well, of course, the cottage has the same family associations for him as for Pascal. It occurs to Cass that he might be a more ready source of information than Pascal, although she doesn't want to pursue the topic now: she must keep a firm grip. Instead, she asks about his interest in birdwatching. It fits oddly with her idea of him as a journalist, frequenting smoky wine bars and late-night parties.

"I do a weekly column for the paper," he explains. "Nature

notes, that sort of thing. It's better than doing weddings and cattle shows. The old codger who used to do it retired last year and I'm the only person who knows the first thing about wildlife. As far as the great reading public knows, it's still good old Jacques doing his stuff every week. That was his pseudonym and now it's mine."

Making sure she's in front when they get to the lake, Cass takes the clockwise path to the lake rather than the other one which passes close to the cottage. As they walk, Philippe alerts her to various bird calls: a nuthatch, a whitethroat. He is obviously knowledgeable.

"We used to hear nightingales here when I was a boy," he says, as if referring to ancient history. "I haven't heard one for a few years now."

"You lived in the village?"

"Yes, till I was about ten, and then we moved away to Carentan when Dad got a job there. When we lived here, he used to bring us in here fishing, me and Pascal. Until Pascal found out about the Jews' house. Then he wouldn't come any more."

They reach the hide. There is someone else in there, an elderly man with a telescope, and he and Philippe exchange notes on recent sightings. It is a calm, still evening, with midges drifting over the lake, the air warm with the scent of honeysuckle. Philippe points out shelduck, a ringed plover, a solitary greenshank, and scribbles brief details in a lined notebook. After an hour – he meant that precisely, Cass notes, as if he rations out his time among several important callings – he closes his book and puts it in the pocket of his chambray shirt. "Right. Time to go, I think."

They walk back to the stableyard, this time taking the path near the cottage. Cass is no longer afraid – Philippe is so brisk and practical that she doesn't expect to find herself behaving oddly. He doesn't even glance at the cottage, but she risks a look back and sees its shattered roof rising above the apple blossom, its hanging shutters and blank eye of window. With Philippe striding ahead of her, it is just a deserted cottage.

Back at the yard, he says, "What now? I'm hungry, are you? How about going somewhere for dinner?"

"All right," Cass agrees cautiously.

"Bayeux? It's crammed full of British tourists, especially this time of year, but I know a nice restaurant that doesn't get too packed."

"I'll have to go and change," Cass says, still wearing her work clothes that smell of horse and lawn-mowings.

"OK, no hurry. Wear that nice cream thing you had on the other night."

For the second time she finds herself running upstairs while Philippe waits. He took it for granted that she would accept, she reflects. Ignoring his instruction about what she should wear, she has a quick shower and puts on leggings and a denim shirt. She brushes her hair loose and cleans her teeth, deciding not to bother with make-up. She wonders again whether Pascal has suggested to Philippe that he should take her out. She hopes not; she doesn't want Philippe to do her any favours. Not that he gives the impression of doing anything he doesn't want to do.

So that he won't have to bring her back afterwards, she drives to Bayeux in her own car. They find parking places near the tapestry museum and then Philippe takes her down a narrow, paved side-street with the towers of the cathedral soaring above. The restaurant is small and dark; although it is quite early there are already a few local people drinking at the bar. Two or three of them, including the bar waiter, greet Philippe as he comes in. Cass can tell that he likes appearing with a new female companion; doubtless he is used to it. He doesn't introduce Cass but asks what she would like to drink and leads the way to a corner seat.

After a few drinks – Cass switching prudently to mineral water – they move to a restaurant table and the waiter comes for their order. It is an unpretentious place, with checked tablecloths and raffia mats, crusty bread in a basket, music loud enough to be in the foreground rather than the background.

"Is this a local journalists' haunt?" Cass asks.

"We come here quite a lot, yes," Philippe says. "It's handy after work. For pushing the boat out there are posher places in Bayeux."

Cass asks how long he has been in his present job and he tells her about his ambition to be a journalist for a national paper. "I want to travel, see the world. I mean, nothing against Pascal, I get on with him really well, but he's an idiot to have settled down so young. Married at twenty-two, a father by twenty-three."

Cass dislikes the critical tone he adopts when talking about Pascal. She has noticed it already this evening, although there was no trace of it on Saturday night when Pascal was present.

"You don't think it was the right thing to do?" she asks.

Philippe breaks a piece of bread. "He didn't have a lot of choice. Gilles was already on the way. Our parents were furious at the time – Dad called Pascal all kinds of fool. But Pascal was quite definite about it. He was going to get married."

Cass is guiltily aware that she wouldn't like Pascal to know they're talking about him like this, but is too curious to change the subject. In any case, Philippe doesn't need much encouragement. The food arrives – oysters for Philippe, goats' cheese and salad for Cass – and he continues: "Monique's great, and they're happy together – as I'm sure you saw for yourself. But Pascal's never going to make any money. That printing business is on its last legs, even they admit that. And now the horses. Pascal likes the work better than the printing, that's why he does it. But it pays a pittance."

"Does that matter, if they're happy?"

Philippe grins. "It wouldn't suit me. Scraping a living."

"I don't suppose local journalism pays a fortune, either."

"No, but this is only the start. I've got big ideas."

Watching him, Cass is sure he has. He refills her wineglass and his and she forgets to say that she doesn't want any more. She watches her hands cupping the glass as if they belong to someone else. She thinks: I am having dinner with a good-looking French journalist. What would Robbie say, or Amy? It sounds more exciting than it actually is. If she had never met Pascal, she would doubtless be highly pleased with the situation. But she *has* met Pascal, she can't have him, and no one else will do. She likes Philippe less now than she did on Saturday, and not only because he isn't Pascal. On closer acquaintance, his self-assurance is less appealing.

"I should think it's pretty deadly for you," he remarks "holed up there with your old uncle and aunt, isn't it?"

"No, I like it. It's not as though I'm living in the house with them."

"That really would give you the creeps. Knowing wha went on there. I suppose you *do* know?"

"Some of it." She gazes at him, fascinated. He will tell he whatever he knows. She only has to ask. He won't clam up like Pascal does, because he doesn't feel things as deeply and doesn't expect anyone else to.

"I mean, for a start, you and I could have been relations. Di you know that? My grandfather was going to marry your aunt."

"Yes. I did know." She raises her wineglass and swallow more than she meant to. "Why did they break it off?"

"You don't know?"

She tries not to betray her eagerness. "There are all sorts o possibilities, aren't there? But no, I don't know, not really."

"Well –" Philippe looks cautious for the first time. "Per haps I shouldn't tell you. She is your aunt – great-aunt – afte all."

"Oh, please!"

"All right." He lowers his voice. "They broke it off becaus she was pregnant."

"By your grandfather?"

"Of course not. By one of the Germans billeted up there in the house. She was going to have a Nazi baby."

"No! That's not true!" Cass stares at him, her hea swimming as she tries to take in this impossible idea. She half-afraid that Philippe's face will melt and dissolve an become someone else's.

"How do you know it isn't?"

"Because Tante Eugénie has never had a baby. Hasn't got any children."

"No, but that doesn't prove anything. My guess is she found somewhere to have a back-street abortion. Isn't that what you'd have done?"

"How can I say what I'd do?"

"You can guess what it would have been like to be pregnant by a German, after the Liberation. She got rid of it," Philippe says matter-of-factly.

"But you don't know any of this!" Cass is sure he is embellishing the story, with a journalist's instinct for sensation.

"True. I only know what I've heard. You know how it is in a small village like St Privat where nothing much changes – people live in the past. Resistance stories are passed around, everyone wants their bit of glory even if all they did was spit at the Germans behind their backs."

The main course arrives, *cassoulet* with scalloped potatoes. Philippe pours more wine. Cass can only pick at her food, turning over Philippe's theory in her mind. She wonders whether Pascal believes it too. If so, he would never have told her something so disturbing; she knows how he puts up shutters, as if it's painful for him. It is part of Duclos family history, after all, though Philippe might just as well be talking about complete strangers.

Absent-mindedly, she drinks her wine, remembering what Yvonne Lepin said about Tante Eugénie disappearing suddenly: it does seem to fit. And perhaps it's better than Cass's own version, that Tante Eugénie ran away in remorse after betraying the Jewish family. Perhaps it was nothing to do with the Jews after all? Not all German soldiers were callous monsters. While Cass can't imagine why anyone would deliberately send the Jews to their deaths, she can sympathize with Tante Eugénie for falling in love and getting pregnant. She thinks of the frightened girl of twenty: alone, in trouble, leaving the village with her secret. Where could she have gone?

"Cheer up," Philippe says. "It was all more than fifty years ago. It's not going to make much difference now, is it?"

15. Robbie

At the end of the meal Cass drinks three cups of strong coffee to counteract the wine she has unintentionally been drinking. The waiter brings the bill and she offers to pay her share, but Philippe slaps his hand over the printed slip to stop her from picking it up and says, "We'll go halves next time, if you like. This is my treat."

Cass notes the *next time*. They walk through the shadowy streets to the car park, past the floodlit cathedral. She has her keys out ready and when they reach her parking place she darts round to the driver's door and says, "Thank you very much. And for the birdwatching. I enjoyed it." She is not sure this is strictly true, and suddenly she wants to get away from Philippe.

Philippe laughs, standing with his hands in his pockets. He must know why she's made a sudden dash out of reach, but doesn't seem in the least offended. "I'll see you again then, Cass. Drive carefully."

She pulls away and drives through a maze of narrow streets and one-way systems to the ring road. Her hands on the wheel and gear-stick are behaving quite normally but she feels dizzy, removed from herself, as if watching someone else drive. Away from the ring road, which is busy even at this time of night, the country lanes are quiet, deserted. The headlights pick out the foam of cow-parsley on the verges. Trees loom, thrusting themselves into the car's path, and hedges tower high. Cass realizes that she really has had too much wine. If she has an accident, now, and hurts someone, she will be just as bad as Robbie, or Kelvin. She didn't mean to drink so much and it was Philippe who kept filling her glass, but it would be no use trying to blame someone else if she did have an accident. She is responsible for her own actions. She slows down, and now the eeriness of the summer night reaches her, the sense of being totally alone in this moving capsule. If she stopped and got out now and walked across the fields, she could disappear. The engine sound gets inside her head and booms around her ears. She might as well be in a space-ship, travelling into the night, as if she can go on and on driving for ever, not knowing where she's going.

All the same, her brain is on auto-pilot, ensuring that she takes the route back to St Privat. Coming from the Bayeux direction she passes the main entrance to Le Clos d'If and sees the house in darkness, the inky yew tree stretching out its branches to cover the windows. Le Clos d'If. It's a good name for the house, sounding closed, cloistered, shut away. Cut off from the village, from people who want to gossip and speculate. Concealing its secrets.

Cass drives round to the stableyard gate. Her relief at getting home safely fades as she switches off her headlights and is plunged into total darkness. She wishes she had thought of leaving the yard lights on so that she wouldn't have to get out of her car into the thick, dark night. There isn't even a light from the holiday flat; the English people must be asleep. Unwilling to get out, she sits in the driver's seat. She thinks of her childhood nightmare that something will brush against her face in the darkness, that a voice will sound in her ear. She remembers needing to go to the toilet but lying in bed terrified, not daring to get out of bed in the dark, and frightened to turn on the light in case the face in her bedroom mirror is someone else's, in case it should break into a grin and speak to her. Childish fears, but still with her now. The terrified child lives inside her.

"Cass! Cass!"

The night is whispering to her. Only the wind in the poplars. She remembers that she keeps a small pencil torch in the glove compartment and reaches for it, hoping the battery still works. Her fingers slide the switch and a small beam of light shines on the dashboard. Now she is afraid of seeing her own face in the driver's mirror, eerily lit from beneath. She gets out of the car quickly and locks up.

With the torch to guide her she unbolts the gate. It gives a whining creak as she swings it open and then shut. She tries to focus on the thin, weak beam of light and to ignore the darkness beyond it, clustering. She only has to reach the door to her stairs and then she can turn on the light, strong electric light to flood out the shadows.

She can smell grass and hay, and hear the rustle of straw as the mare moves in her stable. Safe, reassuring smells and sounds. But there is something else. Something where there shouldn't be something. The sound of furtive movement to the side of the building.

A scream is gathering itself in her throat, pushing up. She knows it is the nowhere girl, come to reproach her, to look at her with her big dark eyes. The nowhere girl will come upstairs with her and into her dreams. Cautiously, Cass moves to the corner of the stable and shines her torch. Slabs of stone, cement. Shadows. Dustbins. Two eyes, green as twin jewels in the torch beam, held for an instant. Then a flash of rust, a slinky, long-legged dog shape, a plume tail, running fast and low into the shadows. A fox raiding the rubbish bins.

Cass's relief is a bubble of laughter, a gush of exhaled breath. Unafraid now, she walks to the stair door and turns on the light and goes up to her flat.

In her dreams there are night-creatures coming out from the woods, from the scrub, slinking across the grass and around the buildings, like dark, half-hidden thoughts.

"How was the birdwatching?" Pascal asks in the morning.

"Oh – fine, thanks. We saw a greenshank. And we went for a meal afterwards, in Bayeux."

"Really?" Pascal looks as if he'd like to hear more, but at that point Oncle Gérard arrives in the yard on his daily visit. His creased face is anxious and he gives the stallion and the mares no more than a cursory glance before telling Cass, "Your aunt's not at all well, I'm afraid. I'm going to get a doctor out to see her if she's not better tomorrow."

"What's wrong with her?"

"High temperature, feverish. Possibly not serious, but I'm worried in case it turns to pneumonia. She had that a couple of years ago. It takes a long time to get over."

"Shall I come up and see her?"

"She'd like that. She doesn't see many people at the best of times."

After lunch, Cass cuts early roses to take indoors for her aunt. Walking up to the house is like entering its shadow. She doesn't want to go in. There is nothing young and alive in there to push out the air the German soldiers breathed, to drown their voices, drive out the memories. When Oncle Gérard tells her, "She's asleep at the moment. Best not to disturb her," she hands over the roses and walks back across the sunlit lawn, giddy with relief.

Next morning, she is digging out rich compost from the bottom of the heap when Pascal calls her name and comes across the lawn.

"There's someone here to see you."

"Who?"

"Someone English."

"But I don't know anyone English. Only the holiday people."

"He seems to know you."

He? Baffled, Cass brushes her hands together and follows him back to the yard. There, looking in at the mare and foal, is –

"*Robbie!* What on earth are you doing here?"

She does a genuine double-take as he turns to grin at her. It is so unbelievable that he can be here, in France, when he's supposed to be at school in England, that she thinks she must be hallucinating. But it's definitely Robbie: tousled hair, big smile, pleased with himself at having popped up unexpectedly.

"Just thought I'd drop in."

"Drop in!"

They look at each other and there is an awkward moment when Cass thinks Robbie is going to embrace her and that she really ought to hug him or do something welcoming instead of just standing there staring. Then Robbie looks at Pascal.

"This is Pascal," Cass says. "Pascal, this is Robbie – er – a friend, from home."

Pascal shakes hands. "You must have been very much determination to arrive here with no car," he says, in his endearingly clumsy English.

"Yes, I came on the overnight ferry and then hitched. It's taken me bloody ages," Robbie says. "No one had ever heard of this St Privat place. I suppose you're in the middle of working," he says to Cass. "Can you leave off and come out with me?"

Cass can hardly refuse. Pascal, obliging, says in English, "I will manage by myself easily here. If you want to go out all day, Cass, don't worry for this evening."

"All right. Thanks. Do you want to have a look at the horses, Robbie, while I dash up and change?"

Upstairs, she glances out of the window and sees Robbie leaning over the paddock fence with Pascal, looking at the stallion. She doesn't know whether to be impressed by Robbie's enterprise in getting here, or annoyed by his cheek at turning up uninvited. It makes it very difficult for her to say, "Go away, Robbie. I'm not going out with you any more," when he's crossed the Channel especially to see her. For the second time in a week she is preparing to go out, leaving Pascal behind. First Philippe, now Robbie. She doesn't want either of them. They are intruders. This is *strictly*, she tells herself as she pulls on a sweatshirt, just for today.

"What are you doing here?" she asks Robbie again when they're in her car and driving down the lane.

"I'm on study leave, aren't I? It's official. My exams start next week."

His knee is in her way as she changes gear. She remembers his way of taking up all the available space, sprawling his long legs and arms everywhere. He is wearing a baggy ribbed sweater with a yellow T-shirt underneath, jeans with one split knee, big boots.

"Shouldn't you be revising, then?"

"Yes. But I felt like a break. You can overdo it, sticking your head in a book."

"Maybe. I don't suppose you're running much risk of overdoing it."

"Well, no. I'll get by. I usually do."

It feels so odd to be talking to him like this, as if they've never been parted.

"Why did you come?" she asks.

"To see you, of course. Why d'you think? You obviously weren't going to come back to see me. Not even when I asked. You didn't even answer."

He is good at ignoring things he wants to ignore, she knows. But perhaps she is, too. She decelerates as they approach the main road junction. "Where shall we go?"

Robbie shrugs. "To the sea?"

"OK. We'll stop and buy some food for a picnic."

Robbie has never been to France before and is fascinated by the big *Stoc* supermarket, translating the special offer signs and trying out his schoolboy French to ask for things at the *charcuterie* counter. After the shopping they drive on to Arromanches and walk along the cliffs in a stiff wind, Cass pointing out the remnants of the D-Day Mulberry harbour. They avoid discussing anything personal until they are packing away the leftovers from their picnic, when Robbie says, suddenly and reproachfully, "You've been a bit mean, I reckon."

Cass pushes her hair out of her eyes. "Mean? How?"

"Not bothering to write properly or phone, just a couple of postcards. Can't you forget it now, all that accident business? Kelvin's getting done for it and that David Thwaite guy'll be out of hospital soon. It's a bit tough to finish with me just because of that one second of bad luck."

"Maybe."

Cass almost says, *It isn't for that one second. It's for all the other times when you and Kelvin could have had an accident, and only good luck stopped you.* But she doesn't feel capable of judging any more. Guilt, blame: there's such a lot of it about. Robbie wasn't even driving. Who is she to blame him? She's done stupid things herself. Or would have, given the chance.

"But you're still friends with Kelvin?" she adds.

"Yes. It'd be a bit much to desert him at a time like this, wouldn't it? He won't do it again, anyway."

"Well, I should hope not." Cass doesn't comment further. Learning by experience is fair enough, but not when it's as serious as this, when other people's lives are involved. She might forgive Robbie but she will never forgive Kelvin. Especially as she's sure that his biggest concern is the fine he faces, and the driving ban.

She doesn't want to talk about Kelvin any more and Robbie seems glad to drop the subject. They wander back through Arromanches, past the D-Day museum and the flagpoles and down a ramp to the beach. Gold Beach. The scene of a fierce battle in 1944, but today just a seaside beach, with people eating ice-creams and huddling into their coats. Cass and

Robbie take off their boots and socks and walk down over the sand where the tide has gone out. The sand is cool and damp, ridged. Robbie takes hold of Cass's hand and although she knows she ought to let go, she doesn't. In a way it is nice to be with Robbie: he is safe, straightforward, he belongs to her other life where people argue about their favourite bands and skive lessons and fancy each other and giggle and have fun. He is like a kind-natured brother or cousin, someone she's fond of and can trust. But he belongs in her other life, not this one.

They reach the tide's edge and wade in, chilly water rippling at their ankles.

"When are you coming back to England?" Robbie asks suddenly.

Cass stares out to sea, at silver on grey on blue, ruffled by the wind, sliding and merging. It is out there somewhere, England.

"I don't think I am coming back."

"Don't be daft! What about school? What about your exams?"

"I don't care about school or exams any more."

"You're not telling me you seriously want to stay at that farm place in the back of beyond, pushing wheelbarrows about?"

"No. Not for much longer."

"It's not that Pascal guy, is it?"

"No!" Cass flushes hotly. "He's married, and anyway you don't have to assume that it can only be because of some bloke that I want to stay. There are other things –"

Robbie kicks at the water, sending up salty spray. "Well, what? What is there?"

"I don't know. But –" Cass doesn't know how to explain it. England is crowded and dirty, full of traffic queues and litter, video shops, housing estates, burger bars. In England she was only Cass, in France she is both Cass and Cécile. It is easier just to be Cass, but Cécile is bigger and stronger, wanting more, reaching out. Robbie doesn't know Cécile, doesn't even recognize that she exists.

He is waiting patiently. "But what?"

"I don't know. But I don't want to go back to England, not yet. Not for school."

"Yet? What are you waiting for?"

"I don't know. Something."

The questions are hanging in the air while she drifts off into her thoughts and then drags herself back to find words, reasons.

"You seem so different," Robbie says, frowning. "Almost as if you're not quite all there."

They walk up the beach and sit down to brush sand off their feet. Later, they stop at a *crêperie* for coffee and pancakes with apple and cinnamon. In the bright, modern atmosphere, surrounded by crowded tables, conversation is easier. Robbie talks about friends from school, about his college applications, about failing his driving test and saving up for a car of his own. Cass listens, asking after Amy and other people from her own year at school. Occasionally, while he talks, Robbie's eyes rest on her face in puzzlement. She is feeling increasingly guilty but doesn't know what she can do about it.

"You're really not interested, are you?" he accuses her at one point.

"I am. I'm listening." She makes more of an effort, but knows he is right.

In the early evening she drives him back to the ferry at Ouistreham. The ship, *Le Duc de Normandie*, is already being loaded with cars, the ramps down. Robbie turns to her in the passenger seat with a hurt, regretful expression.

"I suppose this is really it, then, if you're not coming back?"

"I'll be home some time to see Mum and Dad."

"I mean you and me. It's finished, isn't it?"

"But it was, before. I told you. I'm sorry."

"Yes, I know. But I thought – oh well, I suppose it's pointless." He turns round to get his rucksack from the back seat.

"I'm glad you came today, anyway," she says, and means it.

"Bye, then." He leans towards her and gives her a quick, clumsy kiss. She hugs him in return and as he moves away she sees tears welling in his eyes. He gets out quickly, slams the door and walks away, head down.

"Robbie!"

She is going to cry too. It's almost too late. If he gets on the ship it will carry him away for ever. She can get out and run after him, tell him she's sorry, she will come back home and things will be as before, and he will give her one of his bear hugs and grin like he used to.

But she doesn't. She can't. She stays in the driving seat, her eyes blurring as Robbie disappears among the other foot passengers and is gone.

16 . Bloodlines

"That was your boyfriend from England who turned up yesterday?" Pascal asks.

Cass is measuring out feeds, leaning into the bins. Soft hiss of oats, the heavier patter of crushed barley.

"He isn't my boyfriend. He used to be but he isn't now."

"I should think," Pascal says, "he must be very keen to come all the way here on the chance of seeing you."

"Well. He isn't my boyfriend any more, all the same."

"You could have a bonfire, couldn't you," Oncle Gérard says, "with all that stuff you've cut out from the shrubbery. Now that it's all dried out. There's a place behind the shed. Easiest way to get rid of it."

Cass drags and carries all the cut growth round there. Twigs bend and snap, dried leaves fly up into her face on brittle stems. The bonfire place is a charred grey circle, dry. Ashes and charcoal, the burnt smell rising up into her nose and mouth. She cuts the longer stems with secateurs, and they spring apart as the blades close through softer wood inside, still green. Still alive. Before fetching paper and matches Cass searches through the twigs and leaves, parting them with her hands, picking out snails, a spider, a ladybird, moving them to safety. She has a horror of living creatures being burned alive.

Easiest way to get rid of it. Lit, the first piece of screwed paper curls and untwists, writhing, the flame blue then yellow, taking hold and spreading. Dried twigs crackle as the fire gains heart. She can smell the burning wood, the bonfire smell of childhood, autumn, Guy Fawkes' nights in friends' gardens. Wisps of smoke curl into the clear air and dissolve. There will soon be a new layer of crumbling grey ash on the ground.

Tante Eugénie is no better today, the housekeeper says, when Cass makes her duty visit in the afternoon. She is staying in bed all day but has told Madame Gautier that she wants to see Cass if she comes up to the house. Reluctantly, Cass climbs the polished wooden stairs, past a windowsill halfway up with a big vase of flowers and a view over the fields and woods. She would rather be outside.

She knocks on her aunt's bedroom door, as directed by Madame Gautier, and goes in.

Tante Eugénie is half-propped up on a bolster and pillows in the big bed. Her hands rest on the bedspread, the rings too heavy for frail fingers. She looks small and defeated, as if she has surrendered. Tired eyes look at Cass and a smile stretches her dry lips in a way that looks almost painful.

"Cécile. Thank you for coming." Tante Eugénie raises her head slightly. She speaks with an effort, her voice hoarse. "And for the flowers yesterday."

She is wearing a white embroidered nightdress and bedjacket, in a fresh light fabric. Against the piqué edging her collarbone juts, the skin of her neck sagging. Without the make-up she usually wears it is as if she has taken off a mask. The face beneath is naked, vulnerable, years older. The most vibrant things in the room are the flowers Cass sent in yes-

terday, their colours glowing against the dark wood of Tante
Eugénie's dressing-table. The room smells of flowers and
talcum powder and something else underneath. Cass want to
run away, back to the horses and the garden and her work.
She sits in an upright cushioned chair beside the bed, wondering how soon she can leave. On the bedside table she
notices Tante Eugénie's rosary beads and her missal with its
ribbon marker. There is a crucifix on the wall opposite.

Tante Eugénie settles back against the pillows. "I'm glad
you came up, Cécile. You're a good girl."

"I'm not," Cass says.

But Tante Eugénie doesn't seem to hear. She continues, "I
wanted to talk to you alone. To explain things."

"What things?" Cass is afraid of her aunt, of her illness, of
her secrets, in this enforced intimacy.

"Why I brought you here."

One of Tante Eugénie's hands is clutching and releasing a
handful of the bedspread, like a cat kneading, seeking purchase. Her eyes are half-hidden behind hooded lids.

"There's no secret about it, is there?" Cass's voice sounds
too loud and too strong, as if she has no right to be young and
healthy in this quiet room where age and sickness float like
dust particles in the air. In the air she breathes. If she stays
here they will infect her too and she will become pale and ill,
smothered between starched sheets, pressed and pinned
down like a butterfly in a collector's case.

"There was more to it than that. Gérard needed help with
the horses and garden, yes, but I had other reasons besides."
Tante Eugénie's eyes are completely closed now, the lids
papery and veined, like dead leaves. "I wanted you to come

here, Cécile, because I wanted to see you before it was too late. So that I can imagine you living here, turning it into a family home again, a happy place with children, like it used to be. This house will be yours one day."

And her eyes suddenly open and fix themselves on Cass's face, shrewd, waiting for a reaction.

"Mine? But why should it be mine?"

"It is for you," Tante Eugénie says, "because you are my granddaughter."

Cass stares at the bony hand clutching the bedspread, pale skin against whiteness, fingers like twigs. She hears what Tante Eugénie says but can't attach any meaning to it. The words don't make sense.

"But I'm not," she says dully. "How can I be? I'm Grandmère's granddaughter."

There is something out of her reach, darting and flashing above the slow muddy spiral of her thoughts.

"No," Tante Eugénie says hoarsely. "We changed places. Grandmère – Jeanne – is your great-aunt. I'm your grand-mère."

"Changed places?" It sounds like a game. "I don't understand."

"Have you never guessed?" In spite of Tante Eugénie's tiredness and ill-health, there is enjoyment in springing her surprise, in the power of knowledge. "Your mother is my daughter. Thérèse is my daughter."

"But I don't understand," Cass repeats. "You and Oncle Gérard haven't got any children. How can she be your daughter?" Is Tante Eugénie going gaga, she wonders, imagining things, making things up?

But the eyes that scrutinize her show no hint of confusion or senility. "Gérard hasn't, no. But I have. I have a daughter, Thérèse. When she was born I gave her to my sister Jeanne, in England. And Jeanne brought her up."

"Why? Why would you give away a daughter? Why hasn't Mum ever told me?" Cass feels stupid; there is something here she is supposed to understand.

"Thérèse prefers to avoid the truth. She knows, because I have told her myself. But she prefers to believe that she really is Jeanne's daughter. That's why – have you not noticed? – she won't come here more than she feels obliged to, rarely writes. And that's why she won't have the house when I – when I die, and Gérard. That's why it will come to you. My only granddaughter."

"But not Oncle Gérard's." Cass fishes a single fact out of the muddle. "Who is my mother's father, then? Were you married before?"

"It was in the war." Tante Eugénie's eyes close again, tiredly. "You must understand the strains we were under, in a small village like this. We had German officers staying here, in the house – we had no choice in the matter. And I had friends in the village who were working against the Germans, who were hiding prisoners, collecting guns –"

"In the Resistance."

"Yes. One of them my fiancé, Gaston. We were planning to marry. And then, things became difficult between Gaston and myself because of the Germans. I was supposed to listen, report things to Gaston and his friends. But one of the young officers started paying me attentions and Gaston began to suspect that I was telling Resistance secrets to the Germans, instead of the other way round – German secrets to the Resistance."

"But you weren't?" Cass whispers.

The hand is still plucking at the bedspread, pulling it, twisting a strand of tassel around a finger.

"Not then. But – partly for revenge on Gaston – I started to encourage my young German. He was blond, very handsome and tall. Jürgen, a junior officer. He came from Berlin and his two young sisters were killed there by the English bombs. We used to walk in the gardens and fields together."

Cass wants to stop the dry, cracked voice from talking, spilling out its secrets like water trickling over stones. But she can't stop her aunt. She must know.

"And you told him about Gaston?"

"No. I never betrayed Gaston." Tante Eugénie swallows with difficulty. "But – in the spring of 1944 – I found that I was going to have a baby. I asked Jürgen for help. He – Instead of helping me, he tried to blackmail me. He knew about Gaston already, he had found out somehow. And he threatened to have Gaston shot unless I told him the names of the others I knew in the village. Terrorists, he called them, saboteurs. The Germans already suspected there was going to be an invasion. The SS were moving into the area, and they wanted results – there was a suggestion that some of the army had been having an easy time here, holed up in a quiet village like this. The SS were hot on the trail of various Resistance workers and they treated them brutally if they caught them. No matter how little evidence there was. I suppose Gaston alone would have been a catch, but it would have been even more to Jürgen's credit if he could have presented the SS with a whole list of names. But I didn't give him the names."

The room is full of secrets. Whispering, hinting, pushing their way out of the past and into the present, breaking the air's surface like seedlings pushing up through earth.

"You told him something else instead?"

Cass can hardly force the words out, her voice as hoarse and faint as Tante Eugénie's. She knows the answer already. She knows what her aunt told the German officer, to save Gaston.

"I told him, yes," Tante Eugénie says, in a flat, drained voice. "About the family hiding in the woods, a Jewish family. And that is what I have had to live with ever since."

Words. Floating into Cass's brain and lodging there, like slow-release drug capsules.

"And the baby?" she whispers.

"I ran away. I left home. I couldn't let anyone know about the baby. There were rumours already, about the Liberation. The Germans soon left the house, in retreat, driven back. I thought of making Gaston believe the baby was his, but – the timing didn't make that possible. Before the British soldiers came I was out of the village, staying in a town on the Loire. I made up a story about my husband having been killed in the *Maquis*, and people were kind to me. And then I went to England where my sister Jeanne was already married. She agreed to take the baby from me, to avoid a disgrace. It wasn't the baby's fault." She looks at Cass. "I wasn't the only young woman in France to be left with a half-German baby. That was one of my secrets. The other was worse."

Yes.

"But you can put it right, Cécile," the cracked voice whispers. "You must live here and marry and be happy. I want to be able to think of you. This house has been silent for too long."

Cass wonders if Tante Eugénie is going to die. She looks frail enough to die, as if the life is being slowly pressed out of her by the weight of the sheets and the blankets. Cass imagines her becoming thin and transparent like tissue and then fading away altogether. Her bluish lips move silently in what seems to be a prayer, carrying on another dialogue in the intervals between her remarks to Cass. She has talked as if telling the truth about the past can relieve her of guilt. As if she can hand it over to Cass.

"It was the choice I was given," Tante Eugénie whispers, so closely that Cass has to bend closer to hear. "Gaston, who I still loved, or a Jewish family who meant nothing to me."

She doesn't expect an answer. Her eyes are closed, her lips continue to shape the words of the prayer: *Holy Mary, Mother of God, pray for us sinners now and at the hour of our death.* Slowly, her lip movements become vague, twitching rather than forming words. Her breathing deepens and Cass realizes that she has fallen into a doze.

Cass looks at the sleeping face of the old woman. She looks harmless now, an elderly lady who might concern herself with knitting or books when she wakes up. No longer terrifying. But Cass can't bear to stay in the room a second longer. The dust and the secrets are choking her, teeming into her lungs, getting in through her skin. She is on her feet and out of the room, forgetting to close the door, running downstairs dizzily. She is literally a different person from the one who climbed up. Through the hall, her feet skidding on the rug, out into the sunshine, taking great gulps of the spring air.

She is no longer Cass, half-English and half-French. She is the granddaughter of a German soldier. She is the granddaughter of the German officer who sent the Jewish family to their deaths.

The house has claimed her.

She has to get away. Across the lawn, her feet pounding, as if sheer speed and energy can shake off the clutch of the house and her aunt. Gasping into the yard, up the stairs to her flat. Looking wildly around, grabbing a purse, her rucksack, a sweater and waterproof. Snatching up her car keys. Out through the yard gate, bumping into someone coming in.

"Cass? Where are you – ?" Mouth and eyes in a surprised face. She pushes past and runs to her car. Throws her rucksack into the back seat, fumbles with the keys. The engine starting first time, thank God. A hand reaching out to the driver's door, a startled face looking at her, the mouth saying something. A face she knows vaguely. She pushes the catch down and reverses quickly, jerking Pascal away from the car. Bumping away down the track, she looks in her mirror and sees him standing there staring after her. Helpless. She has escaped.

The other face is still there, wan and still against the pillow, the mouth spilling out its terrible secrets. The voice whispers in her ear. *Put it right, Cécile. Put it right.*

How?

Tante Eugénie has put everything wrong.

It is too late, too late by more than fifty years. The nowhere girl is nowhere. She is burned fragments of ash drifting slowly down to earth, settling. If she is anywhere she is in the grass, the trees, the sky.

What is her name?

Cass is driving fast, too fast. Where to? She doesn't know, letting the road take her, the curve and bend ahead drawing her on. Left or right at a junction? She lets her instincts decide. It doesn't matter anyway. Away from Le Clos d'If, away from her great-aunt who is really her grandmother.

Perhaps none of it is true. Perhaps Tante Eugénie is rambling, hallucinating. Perhaps it runs in the family.

But her own phantoms are real enough.

Mother, daughter, granddaughter. Grandfather. Jean-Luc wasn't her grandpère after all. He was only pretending to be. He wasn't Mum's father. He is no relation to Cass at all. Grandpère, grandmère. Mother, aunt. They are names that can be switched about, handed from one person to another as if you can try them on like hats, swap them if you don't like them. Or play pass-the-parcel. Pass the baby. See who gets it when the music stops.

My mother.

Me.

Cass drives on. *Cédez le passage. Vous n'avez pas la priorité. Bayeux. Port-en-Bessin.* She doesn't know where she is going, or why.

17. Bleeding

The road ahead drops away and between gorse bushes on either side the sea appears to rise, silver-grey, gleaming. To the right, in a dip, a small town. Cass hesitates, not wanting to commit herself to right or left along the coast: to take either direction would be to make too positive a decision. She must stop here.

She parks the car among dunes and gets out. There is a dull ache in her abdomen, dragging downwards. At first she thinks it is the same ache that tugs at her whole body, but then she feels a warm trickle between her legs and realizes that she is bleeding. She has forgotten about the pattern of dates which usually she checks so carefully, the day she marks in her diary with a cross.

Good. She ought to bleed. If only all of it could drain out of her, all the pain and the ache and the guilt. She aches so much that she could bleed for ever and never be emptied of it. In the village she buys what she needs in the chemist's and then finds a sea-front café where she can use the toilet. To justify her visit she orders coffee and sits with it at a table overlooking the beach. It is surprising to find herself doing such normal things: coping with her period, picking up the cup and drinking, her hand gripping the handle. Surprising that she still knows how to do such things. Anyone looking at her would see a girl quietly drinking coffee in a seaside café. They wouldn't be able to see the ache that gnaws inside her and won't let go.

She doesn't know who she is any more. Cécile Angélique Sutherland. Just meaningless sounds, empty puffs of air, dissolving into nothing. Cass, Cécile. There is a third part of her now, invisible but there inside somewhere, stirring and staking a claim. A German part. French, English, and now German as well. She is spread out so thinly that she doesn't exist. She is nowhere. Her body is sitting here calmly drinking coffee but her thoughts are whirling, out of control.

There is a man in Germany who is her grandfather. Jürgen someone. Does he know she exists? Does he wonder about her? Perhaps he has proper grandchildren of his own.

What did you do in the war, Grandad?

I sent Jewish people to be murdered. I sent them to the gas chambers. That's what I did.

Both her grandparents. They both did it. Does he live with his secret as Tante Eugénie lives with hers?

It's Cass's secret too, now. Tante Eugénie has handed it to her and she can't give it back.

Does he go to confession and believe that Holy Mary can intervene and save him? Holy Mary, with her pink plastic face in Tante Eugénie's shrine. Her sweet doll's face with its painted lips. Thousands and thousands of Hail Marys, Tante Eugénie must have said over the years. How many Hail Marys for a life? How many for the nowhere girl? For her mother and father? And that other prayer, or instruction, it sounds like: *Pray for us sinners now and at the hour of our death.* But sinners are everyone. You are a sinner for having impure thoughts or for coveting your neighbour's donkey. I'm a sinner all right, Cass thinks, for having impure thoughts and for desiring Pascal, coveting someone else's husband. It covers everything. Being alive is being a sinner. You can only not be a sinner if you're in a shrine with a painted doll's face. But perhaps there are some things so awful that even Mary has to say, *Sorry, can't help. You're on your own with this one . . .*

Put it right, Cass. Put it right.

I can't. I don't know how to.

It reaches out, spreading and polluting. Tante Eugénie's father, shooting himself because he couldn't bear to know what his daughter had done. That lonely, despairing death after the Germans had gone.

Tante Eugénie's fault.

Cass has finished her coffee but she doesn't know what to do next. So that she can carry on sitting, she orders another cup and drinks it slowly. She doesn't really want it. It is bitter, heavy in her stomach, making her feel sick. She feels dizzy. All she wants to do is to lie down and sleep, a sleep without dreams. But she can't do that here, and anyway she would have to wake up again and fit back inside her skin. It hurts, being in this strange new skin.

An English family comes into the café, a young couple with two small children. The father orders two coffees, a Coke and a milk shake in very bad French. When they sit down, the café is filled with their laughter and their happiness. A family on holiday together. The sort of family Tante Eugénie wants to live at Le Clos d'If, to chase away the ghosts. Where am I supposed to get a family from? Cass wonders. Who does she expect me to marry, for God's sake? I love the wrong person and I've got too much family already, relations I don't know and who have never heard of me. Perhaps Tante Eugénie ought to find a cheerful, happy family like this one and give them the house as a present. Cass doesn't want it. If she went to live there, the ghosts would stay with her.

She doesn't even want herself any more. Her different selves.

Paying her bill, she leaves the café and walks out past the dunes and down to the beach. It is evening, the sun melting into a hazy sunset, the sea calm. It is so totally at odds with Cass's feelings that she would prefer a violent electrical storm, and waves pounding at the shore. Only two hours ago she was in Tante Eugénie's bedroom. Only a little longer before that she was scrubbing out water buckets and chatting to Pascal. Her old self.

Pascal.

Pascal, whose grandfather's life was bought by Eugénie's guilt. She paid for Gaston's life with the deaths of the Jewish family. Otherwise Pascal's grandfather would have been shot and Pascal would never have existed. Lives for lives. The German officer gave one life and took the others in return. Mum's life, Cass's life, in exchange for the nowhere girl's.

The waves are lulling, mesmerizing, their sound filling her head and washing it clean. She could stay here. She can walk out now, into the sea, and not come back. That would seem right. The nowhere girl dissolved into fire, air and earth, Cass into the sea. All the elements, consuming them.

She takes off her shoes (why? she wonders; does it matter if her shoes get wet, if she's going to drown?) and then walks up to her ankles in the water. It is cold then warm, lapping, cool as it touches dry skin higher up her calves. She thinks of the water rising slowly up her body. She will swim out as far as she can and then stop trying and let the waves take her. What will finally kill her? The cold? Will she become unconscious first. Or will she struggle for her last breath, pulled under by the current, until she has to open her mouth and let the water into her lungs to fill and press until the blood roars in her ears?

Is that what it was like for the nowhere girl? Not water but cyanide gas, filling her lungs, choking her?

At least I can choose. I am choosing this. The nowhere girl didn't have a choice.

She steps forward, soaking her jeans. Cold water rises up her legs, her stomach, her chest, making her catch her breath. She leans into the water and swims, her arms and legs making automatic movements. Even now she can't stop herself from trying to swim well, thrusting forward strongly. Salt water splashes into her face as the waves swell around her, dark green, foaming, not silver-grey at all. The pull of the sea frightens her, the hugeness of it and the deep surge from underneath. She dips her face under the surface, just once, sees a swirl of bubbles in the green and her own arms sweeping, feels the sting at her eyes, and knows that she isn't brave enough to do it, to carry on swimming out, and then to stop swimming. Her body won't let her give it up to the sea. The instinct to live is too strong.

If you die now, one part of her mind says to another, *the nowhere girl will die again, with you. Because she only lives in your head.*

Defeated, she turns and swims back to shore, suddenly frightened in case the sea takes her after all, pulls her back and under, takes away her choice. She holds up her head and strikes forward, stumbling on the sand as it rises beneath her and lifts her to safety. Her legs are wobbly and she nearly stumbles with the unexpectedness of her own weight, unsupported by water. She picks up her shoes and walks back to the dry sand. Drowning takes more courage than she possesses. She is too weak.

Two people are walking along the tideline, hand in hand, a young couple. They look at her curiously as she walks up from the sea dripping, carrying her shoes, and she hears the man laugh. They think she is mad. Mad as in eccentric, peculiar. They don't know she's a different kind of mad. There is a fountain of grief rising up inside her, springing out of her eyes. If she let it it would burst out of her mouth in great sobs, the child inside her demanding to be heard and taken notice of and comforted. Because of the laughing couple and the people walking dogs farther up she holds it in, until it's like drowning after all, the pressure pushing up against her throat, beating against her ears. Salt in her mouth, in her nose, running down her cheeks, tears mixing with sea water, trickling under her chin and down her neck. There's an ocean of tears inside her struggling to get out. She imagines herself crying and crying, dripping and dripping, blood and tears and sea water, never getting dry, like someone from a legend. A snail-trail behind her as she walks.

It is like watching someone else crying. It's a relief to let go but it has nothing to do with her. The sobs rise and heave and she watches, sorry for herself crying. But it makes no difference. She will have to stop weeping eventually and be calm and think of something to do, since she isn't brave enough to let herself die. She will have to do something, be somewhere. That's what you have to do, when you're alive. You can't get away from yourself.

In the end she goes back to the car and dries her hair on her sweater and then puts it on. She won't get dry, not tonight. It is almost dark now, with only the palest streaks of reddish light over the sea. She is in her car, her own little piece of territory. Her hands take over. She watches them start the car engine, switch the heater on full, turn the steering wheel away from the coast. She is going to Ouistreham, she realizes. The ferry sails every night and several times each day, and has done since she's been in France. Every night she could have got on it and gone home.

The narrow roads by the coast, easy to follow in daylight, are a baffling maze by night. The names of villages she's never heard of leap at her in the car headlights, pointing imperiously. The arrows keep diverting her inland. At last she sees the signs for the car ferry and knows that she's going to make it, not drive round aimlessly all night. Cars are cruising slowly towards the ferry terminal, people coming back from their holidays. She joins the queue, wondering whether she can pay for a ticket at one of the booths or whether this sailing is already booked up.

She glances in the driver's mirror. In the glare of artificial light she looks terrible, hair hanging lank and matted, eyes red and swollen with crying. She looks mad. They'll never let her on the boat like this. And then she thinks of a more practical problem. She hasn't got her passport. It's back in her flat, in one of the bedroom drawers. She hasn't even got enough money.

Instead of being disappointed, she is almost relieved. She doesn't really want to go home anyway, she realizes. It's not her home any more. That was Cass who lived there, the old

Cass who went to school and to parties and went out with Robbie. That was a different life, hundreds of years ago. Perhaps the old Cass is still there, back at school, visiting her friends, not knowing that Cécile is stranded over here in France. Cass is still a perfectly normal sixth form girl. It's Cécile who's going mad.

There's Mum at home too, Mum whom she doesn't know how to face yet. The new Mum who is half-German, Tante Eugénie's daughter.

Anyway, she definitely can't get on the *Normandie*. That's decided for her. She gets a brush out of one of the side pockets of her rucksack and makes an attempt to tidy her hair, just for something to do. It is stiff with salt but at least she can get the tangles out. She sits in the queue for a bit longer, because she's not sure how to make the difficult manoeuvre of getting out of the line, reversing round and going back the wrong way. When she tries it, people hoot and stare and mouth words at her, crude English words. But she's away, and free, heading away from the terminal, towards Caen and the night.

She isn't going back to Le Clos d'If or the stables, she knows that. She sees herself in the Fiat Panda, a tiny yellow dot on the map of France, like a yellow beetle eating its way into a leaf. She will go anywhere but there. Le Clos d'If is a black hole that will suck her in if she goes near enough.

18. Damage

Whichever way she tries to go, the place is drawing her back. She goes all the way into Caen, round the endless ring road and out again, turning and winding down country roads until she has lost all sense of direction. And then she finds that the signs still say the same. Bayeux. Juvigny. Villers-Bocage. She is going back like a homing pigeon. The cottage waits there in the woods, hollow and empty, its broken roof open to the dark sky. Calling her.

No!

She resists the road to St Privat and turns towards Villers Bocage, Villeneuve, Tilly-sur-Seulles. Her eyes are heavy with tiredness now, the road blurring in front of her. The car heater warms her but her clothes are still damp and clammy and the cuffs of her sweater cling to her wrists. She can't drive all night and anyway the needle on the petrol gauge is pointing to low. In her purse there's enough money for a little petrol, but what then? And she's hungry, not having eaten since lunchtime – lunchtime yesterday, it must be by now. Her body keeps making its insistent demands. I want food. I want sleep.

What will she do when she has no money left?

Perhaps, tomorrow when it's light, she will have to make a quick raid on the flat, to collect dry clothes and her cheque book and passport. At least then she will have more freedom. But she still doesn't know where she will go. And now –

A lay-by opens up at the side of the road, a picnic place with tables and a rubbish bin. She pulls over. It will be uncomfortable but at least she can sleep here in the car. Just for a few hours. Her watch got wet in the sea and has stopped, but it can't be many hours till dawn.

When she turns off the headlights, the darkness settles around her, thick and choking, pressing against her ears. The silence shrieks at her. If she sleeps, the silence and the darkness will go away. Uncomfortably, she arranges herself across the two front seats. It's too narrow to lie down properly but she is so tired that she thinks she will sleep anyway. And then she thinks of someone coming to the car while she's asleep, looking in at her. Stirring, she pushes down the door catches but is unable to banish the thought of faces at the window, staring in. She fidgets restlessly. As the warmth from the car heater fades, she starts to shiver in her wet clothes. Her feet are numb.

It's no good.

She will have to keep going.

Raising herself stiffly, she settles back in the driver's seat and rubs her hands over her face. Her eyes sting from salt and crying and fatigue. She hasn't even got her pencil torch – she left it up in the flat the other night, forgetting to bring it back to the glove compartment. She fumbles with the keys and the engine starts.

On the road again, gaining speed. Automatic reactions taking over.

She can't be far from the next town now, although what difference can that make? She will have to drive straight through –

Headlights piercing the night, coming straight for her, a horn blaring *Get out of my way*. Too late, as she wrenches the wheel to the left, she realizes that in her exhaustion she has forgotten to drive on the right. The other vehicle looms, flashes past. She is swerving out of control, her hands heaving at the wheel, to get back on the road. Stems of grass, each one picked out sharply in the headlights, the umbrella-heads of cow-parsley, a hedge in full leaf. She has time to notice all these things, as if she's a detached observer. The hedge rears in front of her as if the car will take off and sail over it like a Grand National runner. But the car refuses. It bucks and tilts, plunges nose-down and comes to rest, jerking her forward. The seat-belt slams like a solid bar against her chest and her head thuds the windscreen. The other car has vanished into the night.

Her brain reels sickly. Everything's in the wrong place, the steering wheel below her, the seat behind and above, the roof dipping. She thinks of turning off the engine and getting out. Her weight makes it difficult to unfasten her seatbelt and the driver's door opens at an awkward angle, upwards. She clambers through, clinging on as it tries to sway back. It's too dark to see what damage the car has suffered but the ground beneath her feet slides away and she realizes that it's wedged nose-down in a ditch. Her legs give way and she sits down in the long grass, clutching at the ground. She takes stock of her body. Everything seems to be still there, nothing broken or bleeding. It's just that she's been thumped in the chest and socked over the head. When she runs her hand over her forehead she can feel a rising dome, bruised and tender to the touch. To her probing fingers it feels like a gross distortion.

She could have killed someone. She could have killed herself, driving on the wrong side of the road in the darkness.

She has survived. Again.

The night is scented with damp grass and earth and honeysuckle, soothing to her jolted senses. But she can't sit here. The grass is wet, its damp coldness already spreading through the seat of her jeans. And she's not sure the car has survived. She can't tell, but groping her way back to its rear wheels she finds them hanging in the air. She won't be able to back out of the ditch, not in the dark, on her own.

She will have to walk.

She reaches inside for her rucksack and finds it on the floor. Then she locks up and starts to walk along the road, towards the town.

The road surface guides her feet, holding her up. As her eyes accustom themselves to the darkness she can see the roofs of the buildings ahead clustered against the sky, and a church spire. It has become her goal, reaching the town, although she has no idea what to do when she gets there. Walking is the most tremendous effort, as if dragging herself against some powerful force that pushes her back at each step. Streaks of rosy grey begin to lighten in the sky to the east and she can see the road now, its grey glint, and her feet walking, hauling themselves forward. They're like someone else's feet, going somewhere. It would be easier to sit down in the grass and let herself pass out. Weariness is like a drug, creeping over her body, weighing it down, paralyzing her. One step and then another step. Keep going. If she looks down at her feet for twenty steps and then looks up at the town again, she can see that she's making progress.

Houses now, by the side of the road, isolated houses with big gardens. A railway crossing. Overhead wires. One step, another step. Shutters closed, people sleeping inside, warm and comfortable in their beds. A bus stop, advertisement boards, shops. Green tube light round the chemist's sign. A square with pollarded plane trees and benches beneath, a fountain splashing gently, making her realize how thirsty she is. A *Mairie* fronting the square, a florist's, a *bar-tabac*.

She has been here before.

At the fountain she dumps her rucksack and pushes her hands into the cool water and washes her face, moving her fingers gently over the tender bump on her forehead. She bathes her eyes and lets the cool water run down her cheeks and inside her sweater, then cups her hands and drinks, gulping it down. When she's drunk all she can, she shoulders the rucksack and makes herself carry on walking. Her feet take the street to the left, away from the square, and then a residential road, leading downhill. She can get there now. Not many more steps. Her head reels and she imagines the house swimming out of reach, floating away, a mirage. But there it is: behind its low wall, with pots of tulips in the front garden and the black Peugeot standing in the drive. It is the only house she could possibly come to. Pascal's house. Ten more steps to the front door. Swimming through waves of fatigue. Five steps, three, two.

The doorbell rings with a busy, daytime sound, jangling through the sleeping rooms. But no, not all sleeping. A light flicks on above the door, and Cass sees an upstairs curtain pulled back and a surprised face looking out. Feet running down the stairs, the click and scrape of a bolt drawn back. The door opens.

"*Cass!* What —"

Monique, in a striped nightshirt, her hair dishevelled. The baby in her arms, staring at Cass, plump in a blue sleeping suit. Monique's mouth opens as she takes in Cass's appearance. Then Monique's face and the baby's and the wallpaper and the hallway clock slide into each other and whirl in a drunken spiral, and Cass's legs melt as the floor rises up to hit her in the face.

She is sleeping and waking, dreaming, shouting, swimming and drowning. Floating.

Finally she floats down into a bed and opens her eyes and blinks at sunlight through flowered curtains and an African violet on a windowsill. Her body is still here. It is dressed in a white nightdress that isn't hers and lying under a clean duvet. Coming back to life, her body tells her that it aches all over, her head throbbing painfully.

She looks at the room. A wardrobe, an Indian patterned rug. The only thing she recognizes is her rucksack, which is propped against the wall. She realizes that she must be in Pascal's house. In bed. She vaguely remembers being half-carried upstairs, arms around her, Monique's and Pascal's, and then Monique helping her to get her clothes off and putting her into bed and bringing her a hot-water bottle. Monique asking her questions and her own voice mumbling in reply, talking nonsense, probably. How long has she been asleep? She looks at her watch, but its face is misted with condensation and the hands have stopped. She can't remember what day it is.

She needs to go to the toilet. And remembers that she has her period. Sliding her legs from under the duvet, she finds the packet in her rucksack pocket and opens the door to look for a bathroom. She feels drunk. A door swings open to reveal a tiled bathroom, a wall cabinet with a mirror. As she walks unsteadily in, a face swims to meet her. Long, lank hair hanging each side of a battered face. A swelling above one eyebrow, purpling. Eyelids red and puffy. Lips pale, colourless against pale skin. Eyes blank and staring. A dead face.

When she comes out of the bathroom, Monique is bounding up the stairs.

"Cass! I thought I heard you." She takes her arm and guides her back to the bedroom. "How are you? A doctor's coming. You must get back into bed." Her face is concerned, her dark eyes searching Cass's face. "Come on. You're shivering."

Cass lets Monique lead her back and tuck her up. "How long have I been asleep?"

"It's three o'clock. In the afternoon. Pascal's gone to do the horses but I'll phone him there and tell him you're awake. Now lie quietly and I'll bring you a drink. What would you like? Something hot? Tea?"

"Yes, please."

It is such a relief to be looked after, like a child, that Cass feels tears springing to her eyes again. Monique brings two mugs of tea, kicks off her clogs and sits down on the bed to drink hers. She is wearing dungarees and a red T-shirt and striped red socks and looks like someone Cass's own age. Years younger, the way Cass feels at the moment.

"I mustn't tire you with talking," Monique says, "but before the doctor comes, can you tell me what's happened to your face? And where your car is?"

"I – I crashed my car. In a ditch, not far from here."

"And that's when you banged your head?"

"Yes."

Monique frowns. "But before that – were you in the sea?"

"Yes."

"With your clothes on?"

"Yes."

Monique looks at her steadily but only says, "When the doctor's been you can have a hot bath."

"I'm sorry," Cass says. "Dumping myself on you like this. It's a bit much."

Monique waves her hand dismissively. "Pascal was so worried about you," she says, "when he saw you drive out of the yard with – that weird look, was how he described it. As if you didn't even recognize him. Nearly driving over his feet when he tried to stop you. He said he'd seen you look like that once before and he thought you might have an accident, driving."

"Well, I did."

"But you spent all night driving about first?"

Cass nods. She can't explain, not yet.

"Pascal tried to follow you but then decided you must have gone for the ferry back to England. He had to tell your uncle you'd gone, last night when you didn't come back. Because they're responsible for you, aren't they, your uncle and aunt?"

"Yes." Cass remembers sitting in her aunt's room with Tante Eugénie propped up on pillows just like she is now. Yesterday. This time yesterday, that's all it was. "But my aunt's ill. Dying, perhaps."

"No, she's not," Monique says promptly. "Pascal saw your uncle this morning and he said she's much better today."

"Oh, she –" Cass closes her eyes wearily. Her instinctive thought is that Tante Eugénie could at least have done the decent thing and died. Instead, she's handed her guilt over to Cass and then recovered, springing back to health. In another bedroom, the baby starts crying.

"That's Gilles waking up from his nap." Monique wriggles off the bed. "Don't talk any more. I'll come back when I've seen to him. Drink your tea and rest. When the doctor's been you can have your bath and I'll make you something to eat."

Monique goes to Gilles and Cass lies with her face turned to the wall, her eyes burning. It's not fair that she should be lying here between clean sheets with a doctor coming and a mug of tea and the promise of things to eat, and Monique and Pascal concerned for her. The nowhere girl had no one to pick her up off the floor and take her in and look after her. For her there were only the bare confines of a prison camp, the long train journey, the slam of a door, the guards herding her in with the others to the shower room that didn't shower water but poison gas, to choke and suffocate. The guards bolting the door and not caring, treating it as their day's work. The nowhere girl is a face without a name, a face among all the hundreds of thousands.

If I could go instead of her, I would, Cass thinks. And let her come back. The only way I can put it right.

19. Names

Stress, and the depressive effects of glandular fever combined with the shock of the accident, the doctor says, and prescribes rest and sleeping pills.

When he's gone, Pascal comes up to Cass's room to see her, bringing another mug of tea, and a glass of cider for himself. "I saw your aunt this afternoon," he tells her. "She wants you to go and stay there, in the house."

"Oh."

Cass's head spins in panic. She can't go back to Le Clos d'If. If she goes into her aunt's house she will never recover. But she can't expect to stay here, either, dumping herself on Pascal and Monique – she is a nuisance, a lunatic girl who has turned up to disrupt their lives. She doesn't know what to say to Pascal. She has no right to be here. She must pack her things and go.

"But I don't think it's a very good idea," Pascal continues. He sits on a low chair, still in his working clothes, bringing a warm smell of horses and hay into the room. "Monique and I would both prefer it if you stayed here until you're better."

"Oh, but I can't –"

"It's no trouble," Pascal says. "We've got the spare room. You're obviously in no state to go anywhere. And – well – that house –" He turns the cider glass in his hands. "It was your aunt who upset you so much, wasn't it? Whatever she told you."

Cass nods. She's not sure how much of it Pascal knows

already, and she can't tell him because of his own involvement. He doesn't press her for details.

"I'm sorry for nearly driving over your feet," she says instead.

Pascal smiles. "It's all right. The time before, you hit me in the face. Do you remember?"

"Yes. I'm sorry."

"How do you feel now?"

Cass considers. She has had a bath and washed her hair and taken one of the sedative pills the doctor prescribed. "I don't know. Different. Dopey. I don't think I'm going to hit anyone or do anything else drastic."

"You were shouting out in the night," Pascal says. "A jumble of words – I couldn't hear what. Monique came in to see if you'd woken yourself up but you were still asleep."

Cass vaguely remembers the shouting. "I don't know what about. Things going on in my head, weird things. I hope I didn't wake everyone."

It's so different now, sitting up in bed wearing Monique's sweatshirt and talking to Pascal, noticing the hayseeds in his hair and his tanned fingers against the glass, while the late sunshine shines into the room with a soft, buttery light. She feels more normal, apart from the strangeness of being in bed in the afternoon, in Pascal's house. And then she remembers that Pascal and Monique don't know who she really is. They still think she is just Cass, half-English and half-French. Can she tell them? What will they say when they know?

"I saw her too, once," Pascal says suddenly.

"Saw who?"

"The girl. The girl who was hiding in the cottage. Years

ago, before we moved away from St Privat. Philippe and I used to play in the woods and by the lake and one day – I must have been about ten or eleven – I was hiding from him, in the cottage. She was there, just for a moment, but she stared at me and then darted away. I tried to find her but she'd gone. Afterwards, I knew who she was. That's when my father told me what happened there. Philippe wouldn't believe me, but I knew."

Cass doesn't know what to say. She feels a rush of gratitude towards Pascal. Perhaps she isn't mad after all. Or if she is, then Pascal is too.

"That night when we went to look for the yearlings," he says. "The way you stared at me – it was her."

"Yes."

"And you've seen her too. She's still there."

"Yes. I suppose she always will be."

Pascal looks at her but says no more. Downstairs, there is the sound of Gilles pretending to be a truck, and Monique laughing.

"Monique says you're to stay in bed this evening and you can get up tomorrow if you feel better," Pascal says, as if it's a relief to turn to more everyday matters. "Your car, by the way, has been towed to the garage in Tilly. I saw it on my way this morning and stopped to have a look, and then phoned someone I know who runs a breakdown business. I don't think it's too badly damaged."

"Thank you, Pascal. I'd forgotten all about the car." She is making problems wherever she goes, dumping her car as well as herself. "Do the police know?"

"I suppose in theory we ought to report it," Pascal says.

"But with no other car involved, perhaps it doesn't really count as an accident."

"I'm so sorry to be such a nuisance. I'm hopeless. It must be like having another baby to look after."

"We can manage that," Pascal says, with a slow smile.

"*Worse* than another baby. Babies don't crash cars and leave them in ditches."

"When you're feeling better we'll sort out the insurance details." Pascal looks at her as if unsure whether to ask, but then does. "What did you do, take the bend too fast?"

"I forgot to drive on the right. And another car came along."

Pascal stares at her. "My God, Cass. You must have been in a state."

It is easier to talk about the damage to the car, the horses, the stallion's progress at long-reining. Their conversation is like a small boat bobbing over the surface, avoiding the dangerous fanged rocks lower down. After a while Pascal goes downstairs and Cass sleeps.

The sleeping pills take their effect. Over the next few days, Cass sleeps heavily through swathes of time, waking up in daylight to find that she has slept all night and most of the morning. She can fall asleep at any time of day. In between, she gets up and goes downstairs and plays with Gilles, and talks to Monique and to Pascal when he's there. Pascal brings some of her things from the flat: clothes, her radio, books. But she can't read much yet. Her concentration is too poor.

"Don't rush it," Monique says. "I mean, you have had a sort of – breakdown, really. You can't hurry. The doctor said."

Cass considers the word *breakdown*. Like the car. "But I'm mending now."

"Yes. Slowly."

At Monique's insistence Cass phones home to tell her parents where she is. She only tells them she's not well, not elaborating. Mum wants to come out and fetch her home, but Cass assures her that she's with friends and being well looked-after.

Later, she wonders whether she should have accepted. Monique and Pascal have said she can stay as long as she likes, but she knows she can't lumber them indefinitely. It's not fair. She looks at the accounts she keeps roughly in the back of her cheque book and wonders whether her savings will cover the cost of the doctor's visit and the towing-away of the car, let alone anything else. The cost of these things hasn't been mentioned, but she knows Monique and Pascal haven't got money to spare: Philippe said so. And Monique has been staying at home in the mornings, not going to work at the printer's, presumably to look after Cass.

Cass doesn't want to go home. She doesn't know what she's going to say to her parents about her new knowledge of her identity. But she will have to go somewhere. Face up to things, make decisions. And she will have to go back to her uncle and aunt's, however briefly. She can't just leave; she will have to give some sort of explanation. But not yet: her mind baulks.

In an odd way, she feels more at ease with Monique. With Pascal there are areas best not mentioned, but spending most of the day with Monique, peeling potatoes or trimming beans in the kitchen or preparing Gilles' food, Cass finds it easy to talk about inconsequential things and not have to think too much. Monique doesn't ask questions but lets Cass say as much or as little as she wants.

One afternoon Philippe calls in on his way to an assignment. Cass doesn't know what Monique has told him to explain her presence, but Philippe treats her with caution, as if she might burst into tears or have a screaming fit. They all sit outside in the garden and Philippe plays with Gilles, relaxing as he realizes that Cass is capable of normal conversation.

"You needed to get away from that dreary place," he tells her. "That dreary village where if a dog barks it's the most exciting thing that happens all day. I told you it wasn't doing you any good."

"Listen to Doctor Philippe," Monique teases. "He's got all the answers."

When Philippe gets up to go, he says, "Give me a ring when you're feeling better, Cass, and I'll come over and take you out."

Cass thanks him, although she doesn't really want to go out with Philippe again, and anyway she might not be here for much longer. Monique fetches Gilles's buggy and Cass clears up his toys, and when Philippe has gone they walk together to the local *Intermarché*.

"Pascal says Philippe took you out for a meal," Monique remarks. "Did you get on well with him?"

"Well – it was nice of him to bother. But I don't like him the way I – the way I like Pascal."

She's said it now. The words fall into the space between her and Monique and hang there in the air. *Aimer*: to like, to love.

French doesn't distinguish. Monique's expression doesn't change, but Cass knows that she understands.

"No," Monique says. "I know."

"You knew? You're not surprised?"

"I could see for myself," Monique says, "when you came for dinner that time. And I love him too, so it doesn't surprise me that someone else does."

"I know it's awful and I know it's stupid as well, I mean you and Pascal, anyone can see –" Now that Cass has started on the subject, the words pour out, apology, excuse, denial, she doesn't know what they are.

No, not a denial. There is no need for that.

With wonderful timing she has embarked on the subject just as they reach the supermarket. "It's all right," Monique says. She takes a 10-franc piece out of her purse and gives it to Cass. "Go and find a trolley while I get Gilles unfastened."

They go inside and work their way down the shopping list, pushing Gilles in the supermarket trolley. Cass watches Monique's slight figure as she moves along the aisles, reaching, choosing, turning to Gilles to answer a burbled remark which only she can interpret. The arms pushing the trolley are brown and skinny below the striped T-shirt sleeves and her dark hair swings against her cheek in its bobbed cut which looks schoolgirlish rather than sophisticated. In spite of her small frame and youthful appearance, she has a quiet strength which Cass envies. But she knows that Monique is passing some of that strength to her, and is overcome with gratitude. Monique is the person she needs, to listen and understand and not judge or criticize. Monique is good for her. Cass feels that some instinct has brought her to the person best able to help.

"There's something else," Cass says on the way home, pushing the buggy. "About my great-aunt. She isn't really my aunt. She's my grandmother."

Monique looks at her steadily, not surprised. "Yes."

"You knew that too?"

"Pascal guessed," Monique says. "He knew it must be something like that to make you so desperate to get away. He told me, the night you went, when he was so worried. He knew it must have been something as drastic as that."

"And about the Jewish people," Cass says, her eyes on the swirl of hair on top of Gilles' head in front of her. "That, too."

"Yes. I know."

Cass doesn't know what to say. Monique and Pascal know who her grandfather is, but they're not going to denounce her or throw her out of the house. They don't blame her for it.

For the first time Cass feels alert enough to stay up for a late dinner. To celebrate she and Monique cook the meal together. Mushrooms in garlic, *boeuf en croûte*, cheeses, *crême caramel*. Preparing the food is good therapy, eating it even better. A party for just the three of them. Pascal is the first to tire, yawning over his coffee.

"You go to bed. You've got to get up early." Monique steers him away from the kitchen when he gets up to clear away the dishes. "Cass, too. I'll do this."

Pascal goes upstairs but Cass stays to clear up, and when the washing-up is finished Monique makes more coffee and they settle down at the table to drink it.

"I suppose," Cass says reluctantly, "I ought to think about

going back to England. Now that I'm better and my car's driveable. You'll be needing your spare bedroom back."

"You don't have to go yet. Stay a bit longer," Monique says, and then smiles. "Actually, you're right. We will be needing the spare room. Not immediately, I don't mean you have to go – but some time next year we'll be needing it. It's too soon to be definite yet, and I haven't told anyone else except Pascal of course, but I think we're going to have another baby."

"*Really?* That's great." Cass smiles back and then finds her eyes inexplicably filling with tears. She can't hide them. They well up silently and spill down her cheeks and she fumbles in her pocket for a tissue, not finding one. She thought she had finished with crying but there it is still inside her, a strong unpredictable fountain, ready to gush up and overflow.

Monique gets up and brings a box of tissues from the kitchen and puts it on the table. "Cass? What is it?"

"I don't know. I don't know what I'm crying for. Sorry. I'm really pleased about the baby, honestly I am. You've done so much for me and then you tell me something like that and all I can do is start crying again. It'll be lovely for Gilles to have a sister –"

Monique looks at her alertly. "How do you know it'll be a girl?"

"I don't know." Cass is surprised to realize what she's just said. "But I think it will, I mean *she* will. I'm glad you told me. Your secret, a nice one."

"We'd both like a girl."

"Yes." Cass can see her, a little girl with dark hair like Monique's and a pointed, delicate face.

Neither speaks for a few moments. Cass wipes her eyes and Monique refills both coffee cups. Then Cass says, "My aunt – I mean, grandmother – wants to leave me the house. Put it right, she said. But how can I?"

"It wasn't fair of her to say that. Or to tell you half the things she told you. It was a clearing of her own conscience, but what can she expect you to do?" Monique pauses, turning her coffee spoon over and over in her fingers. "It was the same for Pascal. His father told him about the Jewish family when he was quite young. Too young to be told a story like that. Resistance tales were still being passed around, even then, some of them very exciting and no doubt partly fictional. But this one – Pascal has grown up feeling as you do, that his own life depended on the deaths of the Jewish family in the woods."

"Philippe knew that, too."

Monique glances at her. "Yes, but Philippe can shrug things off. Say it's nothing to do with him so why should he worry? Pascal's more sensitive, like you – more imaginative. He can't shrug it off, even though he's known for years."

Cass reflects on this and knows it's true. Perhaps that's partly why she was drawn to Pascal from the start.

"Even now," Monique says slowly, "if it were up to me, if I could say one word to bring the Jewish family back to life, bring them back from Auschwitz and give them back all the time in between and the lives they would have had, and if that meant Pascal's grandfather was shot instead and so Pascal's father wouldn't have been born and neither would Pascal, or Gilles, or even" – her hand instinctively rests on her stomach – "the new baby, if it meant they'd all have to disappear and never have existed, would I say that one word? I've often wondered that."

Cass doesn't know. An impossible question.

"Fortunately, we don't have to make such choices," Monique says. "It's too big. It's not up to us. We don't have to decide. What I mean is, you don't have to carry it all around with you, what happened in the past. None of it's your fault. That sounds obvious but it's true."

"But what should I do now? I don't know what to do. There are some things I've got to decide. My aunt – I mean, grandmother – telling me those things, as if I could say *It's all right, it's all in the past now, forget it*. Aren't there some things too awful for that? There must be. And *this* must be."

She is thinking of Kelvin as well as Tante Eugénie. But at least Kelvin has another chance. Cass feels the terror of that one moment approaching as if fated, closing in, a moment like others, too soon past and gone, but an instant that can change a life, or lives, for ever. A few words spoken. A bend taken too fast. Cass could have killed someone on the road and have to live with the slow-motion replay in her mind leading to the instant that changed everything. Only luck prevented it.

"Perhaps that's not for you to decide either," Monique says. "If you decide to leave, you don't have to tell her why."

"She'll guess."

"That won't be your fault. Hers, not yours. She chose to tell you." Monique pours more coffee. "It's not easy to see things in black and white. You think what she did was terrible, and it was, but on the other hand you look at her now and see a sick, lonely old woman and that makes it hard to be callous."

"Yes." That's Cass's problem exactly.

"She isn't alone, you know," Monique says. "There are many, many French people with secrets going back to the war. People who got what they could for themselves. People who thought the Germans were going to win and it was best to be on the winning side. People who were threatened or black-mailed. People who just weren't brave enough."

Cass thinks about this. Yes, there were thousands of Jewish people deported, and the family in the woods weren't the only ones to be betrayed. She's not sure that it makes it any better, knowing that.

"Even now, Pascal feels compromised by working there," Monique continues. "He likes your uncle, he likes the stud work, the hours suit him and the job came along at a time when we needed the money, but in pure black-and-white terms he ought to have said no, he wasn't going near the place. If your aunt had anything to do with the horses he would have said no. As it is, he feels uneasy."

"Do you know their names?" Cass asks suddenly. "The Jewish family?"

Monique frowns. "No. I don't think I do. Everyone always called them the Jewish family. But someone must know, in the village."

In the morning it is a real summer's day, the air fresh, with the promise of warmth later. The sky is a clear enamel blue, cloudless. Cass goes out to the paved garden with her crois-sant and coffee and knows that something has changed. She slept well, without dreams, and now her head feels clear, freshly washed-out. Pascal has gone to the stables but indoors she can hear Monique singing to Gilles as she baths him.

It feels to Cass as if she's been wandering about in some shadowy underworld. Like someone in a legend she has come back up, to sunshine and friendship and summer. In the story, she remembers, you only have one chance; you must walk straight out without looking back, or you'll turn into a pillar of salt and stay there for ever. But Cass is allowed to look back. Her underworld is different; it must be known and recognized, because it is still there, and the present is built on it. It is wrong to ignore it, to pretend that the nowhere girl and her family didn't exist. Cass can gaze into the shadows and know what it is like to be lost down there. But she can look forward too.

It's impossible to feel dismal on a day like this. It is summer and she can smell the sharp pungent scents of rosemary and thyme from the pot by the back door and there is a thrush calling somewhere behind the garden wall. There is a new baby on the way, a girl baby. And she has friends now, Monique and Pascal, close friends. She will be going home but she will be back, to visit them. Perhaps to stay in France, to live here.

"You're a real European now," Pascal said to her yesterday. "English, French, German, it doesn't matter much. And it will matter a lot less when you're away from St Privat. We're all European and you're more so than most."

Cass sits on the low wall and spreads her hand against sun-warmed stone. She wonders whether the nowhere girl will go with her when she leaves. She is part of her now. Last night, or rather this morning, going to bed very late, Cass had what seemed at the time a brilliant idea. If Tante Eugénie really does leave her the house, she could give it to Pascal and Monique. They could trim the yew tree back away from the windows and their children's voices could fill the house with fun and laughter, chasing away the ghosts and the shadows.

This morning, it seems the crazy idea it is. Pascal would never want to live there, any more than Cass would. And probably Tante Eugénie won't leave it to Cass after all, now that she's running away.

But the other idea of the early hours is a better one: Tante Eugénie should put up some sort of memorial in the reserve to commemorate the Jewish family and their lives. She must find out their names, if she doesn't already know them; the Jewish family must be given their names back. Then anyone who goes there, through the tangled orchard to the cottage, will know what happened, why the atmosphere makes them shiver and their skin prickle. It shouldn't be a secret any more; it is time for the Jewish family to come out of hiding. It is a small enough thing to do, but Tante Eugénie should be the one to do it and Cass must suggest it to her. You can't change the past and you can't put it right, so the least and the most you can do is remember. With regret, and respect.

Now, she's going to wash up the breakfast things and then walk into town to buy a present for Monique and Pascal. This afternoon Pascal's going to drive her to Tilly to collect her car, and in another two or three days she will go home. And decide what to do, about school, and whether to look for a job in the meantime, and whether to phone Robbie.

"Cass! Look, there's Cass!" Monique is holding Gilles up to the bedroom window, holding his plump arm up to wave.

Gilles is laughing, as if the sight of Cass sitting in the garden is tremendously funny. She waves back, and goes indoors to get on with her day.